One Hundred Shadows

TRANSLATED BY JUNG YEWON

ONE HUNDRED SHADOWS

HWANG JUNGEUN

EREWHON

an imprint of Kensington Publishing Corp.
erewhonbooks.com

EREWHON BOOKS are published by:

Kensington Publishing Corp.
900 Third Avenue
New York, NY 10022
erewhonbooks.com

ISBN 978-1-64566-144-3 (hardcover)

First Erewhon hardcover printing: September 2024

10 9 8 7 6 5 4 3 2 1

Printed in the United States of America

Library of Congress Control Number: 2024932898

Electronic edition: ISBN 978-1-64566-146-7 (ebook)

Interior design by Leah Marsh

여우 비
Yeowoo-bi

lit. "fox rain"

In common with many other cultures, Koreans refer to
a sunshower using this lovely epithet—the meteorologi-
cal phenomenon of rain while the sun shines apparently
indicating the wedding of a fox. The fox's partner varies
around the world; in Korea, the marriage is between a
tiger groom and a fox bride. The Korean kumiho (lit.
"nine-tailed fox") shares many similarities with the
Chinese huli jing and Japanese kitsune, though while
these latter are often depicted as morally ambiguous,
the kumiho is almost always malignant. Using a literal
translation rather than the more prosaic "sunshower"
seemed appropriate for the eerie, shape-shifting nature
of this darkly modern fairy tale.

Introduction

THERE IS AN UNFORGETTABLE, CURIOUS beauty to be found here, in this short book. The novel has elements of fantasy, but it is also at the same time extremely controlled, and realistic in its depiction of its world.

This is a world in which those living on the edges of society, at the very bottom of the social scale, are being brought to the limits of what they can endure. When they reach this point, their shadows rise up, startlingly sudden, and start calling them away from their lives.

It is a world in which, however they choose to deal with these shadows, which seem to offer death an invitation, they find themselves only just barely able to go on with the business of living.

In this dark and dangerous world, a man and a woman are just beginning to love each other. This love, which is so delicate and subtle a thing that at times it seems trembling on the point of shattering, comes to be felt as almost an ethical force, a moral necessity set against the leaden weight of violence of the world which hems these two young people in.

—HAN KANG, JULY 2016

One Hundred Shadows

 *The Woods*

I SAW A SHADOW IN the woods. I didn't know it was a shadow at first. I saw it slip through a thicket and followed it in, wondering if there was a path there, and thinking how familiar it looked. The woods grew more dense the deeper in I went, but I kept on going deeper and deeper because the deeper I went, the more the shadow drew me in.

Eungyo. I turned around at the sound of my name, and found Mujae standing there. Where are you going? he asked.

I was just walking.

Walking where?

I was following someone.

Who?

Them, I said, and turned back to point, but the person I'd been following was nowhere to be seen. Mujae came toward me, pushing aside some branches, and asked what the person had looked like. I'd only seen them from behind, and as I was about to answer it occurred to me that there had been nothing remarkable about the way they'd looked. Small head, narrow shoulders, dark skin, I said.

Like you, Eungyo?

Yeah, like me, I said, and then it hit me. I looked down at my feet, and sensed something odd about the way they were outlined, against the pine cones and white oak leaves splayed over soft soil. My shadow, spread out thin, very thin, stretched out from the little toe of my right foot all the way into the thickets.

My shadow.

And then I understood.

⌒

DON'T GO FOLLOWING shadows, Mujae said, and I narrowed my eyes to bring him into focus, thinking he looked oddly hazy. Yeowoo-bi, I realized, slender as spiders' silk. I stood there unmoving, feeling my eyelids grow heavy with the weight of water. Droplets formed on the tips of my ten drooping fingers. The rain tasted salty on my lips. I stood for a while, despondent.

Shall we head back? Mujae said, turning to leave.

I followed him, the tall grass snapping and crackling as I pushed my way through it. The thickets were so dense that I wondered how I'd managed to come so far in. Now, retracing my steps, the grass and branches are even tougher because they were wet. My trousers and shirt were damp. I rubbed my eyes, wiping away the rainwater that was gathering on my lashes.

Are you crying?

No, I'm not crying. We walked for quite a while like this, but we still couldn't find our way out of the woods.

What should we do?

Mujae stopped and turned to me.

Seems like we're lost.

Should we keep walking?

I don't think we have a choice.

Then let's keep walking for now.

The top layer of the ground, swollen with rain, was so slippery that if you slipped at all, it seemed you'd slip forever. My legs were stinging; I looked down and saw that they were covered with grass cuts. The longest cut was green with sap. Once I was aware of the cuts, my legs stung every time I moved. With my shadow drooping so far behind me I had a hard time just moving my feet, first the left and then the right. Seeing that I was having trouble walking, Mujae came over and took a look at the cuts.

I'm cold, Mujae.

That's because you're standing still.

I feel like I could die.

What do you mean, you could die?

I'm just saying, I feel like I could die.

Is that just your way of talking?

I feel like I could die, that's all.

Mujae wiped away the sap with his sleeve, then straightened up and looked me in the eye.

Should we die, then? Right here, he added, so quietly that I was frightened. I looked at Mujae as if seeing him for the first time. His black eyes peered down at me. His hair, usually somewhat disheveled, had been subdued by the rain.

Eungyo, he said. Don't say you feel like you're going to die, if you don't really plan on dying.

Okay.

Let's keep walking then, Mujae said. He walked on ahead and I followed him. My eyes welled up with tears. Mujae was so heartless, I wanted to let him go on ahead so I could be on my own, but I couldn't do that in these woods, especially when my shadow had risen, so I just kept walking, wiping my eyes.

Are you crying?

No, I'm not crying.

As we were walking our surroundings grew lighter. Mujae stopped and spread out his hands palms upward.

The rain has stopped.

Yeah.

Do you want some gum?

Okay.

Mujae took out a bent stick of gum from his pocket, tore it in half, and handed me one piece. I removed the dampish double wrapper and poked the green-grape gum into my mouth. It was sweet, so sweet that my jaw tingled and my mouth watered. I folded the wrapper neatly and put it in my pocket. I walked on diligently, chewing gum. Each time my wet feet pushed against the ground a deep chill leached up through my soles. I imagined melting away into such a deep chill, becoming a part of these deep woods. Round mushrooms were growing near sinewy tree roots that poked above the leaf mold.

Mujae, I said. Do you think we'll make it out of here?

I'm not sure.

What will happen if we don't?

We'll die, won't we?

Will we?

We'll die anyway, sometime, somewhere, but if we don't make it out of here, we'll die in these woods.

I'm scared.

You are?

Aren't you?

Yes, I am.

Really?

Yeah, Mujae said, still striding forward. I'm scared too, Eungyo.

We walked in silence for a while. The rain had stopped, but the humidity of the sodden woods was stifling. My stomach felt cold even as I walked, moving my body vigorously, and I thought, What do we do if it gets dark before we make it out? Mujae, I said. Tell me a story.

What kind of a story?

Any kind.

I don't know any stories.

Go on, just one.

Hmm, Mujae said. Shall I tell you a story about a shadow?

Why a shadow, of all things?

The mood is right.

I don't want a story about a shadow.

That's the only story I know.

Well, go on then, tell me.

Hmm, Mujae began.

＊

THERE WAS A boy.

Okay.

His name was Mujae.

Hey, Mujae?

Yeah?

Is this story about you?

It's about Mujae.

About yourself, Mujae?

It's about Mujae, I said. Should I go on?

Okay.

There was a boy named Mujae. Mujae's family lived in a large room without a single picture hanging on the walls. There were nine people in the family. A mother and a father, and six older sisters.

Six sisters?

Mujae was the seventh child, the youngest.

That's so many.

Is it?

Why so many, I wonder?

Well, Mujae said, tilting his head a little to the side. They must've liked doing it.

What?

Sex.

I blushed a little, still walking after Mujae.

Eungyo, Mujae said. Is this story too racy?

It isn't racy at all.

Isn't it?

Anyway, it's fine if it is.

Do you like racy stuff?

I said it's fine. My voice sounded tense, and Mujae chuckled.

In any case, for that reason, Mujae's parents had seven children.

So then what happens?

The parents of the boy Mujae probably get into debt.

Probably?

Or inevitably, you could say.

How is it inevitable to get into debt?

Is it possible to live otherwise?

There are people who manage it.

Well, Mujae said, then broke off to concentrate

on negotiating the slope, holding on to tree roots, and went on. I don't really like people who go around saying they don't have any debt. This might sound a little harsh, but I think people who claim to be in no debt of any kind are shameless, unless they sprang up naked in the woods one day without having borrowed anyone's belly, and live without a single thread on their back, and without using any industrial products.

Are industrial products bad?

That's not what I'm saying. A lot of things can happen in the manufacturing process, can't they, when it's the kind of mass production that uses all sorts of materials and chemicals? Rivers could get polluted, the payment for the labor could be too low. What I'm saying is, even if you buy so much as a cheap pair of socks, that low price is only possible because a debt is incurred somewhere along the line.

I see.

In any case, the parents of the boy Mujae get into debt.

Okay.

In this case, the debt is incurred by them signing their name on someone else's document. This is a story about how eventually, after laboring to support a family of nine at the same time as paying back the interest on the debt, only the interest, because the debt itself is far too big, the shadow of the boy Mujae's father rises. It happens on a rainy Friday evening. The boy Mujae is sitting on the edge of the wooden-floored hall, watching the rain drumming pockmarks into the small yard. At that moment, the boy Mujae's father walks into the yard, his shoes muddy and his face pale. The boy Mujae greets his father, but his father just stares at him, then goes inside and lies down. He lies there in silence, even when someone speaks to him, staring up at the ceiling until night falls, then opens his mouth and says that his shadow has risen. He says that he saw the shadow, which had risen before he knew it, as he opened his umbrella in front of a tavern. The boy Mujae hears his mother gasp in fear. Your shadow rose, she says, and did you follow it? Did you follow the shadow? Her voice trembles with fear and the boy Mujae's father nods. How far, how far did you follow it? she asks. Just a little ways, just a little ways. The boy Mujae's mother turns her face away, wiping her eyes. Don't cry, dear, says the boy Mujae's father. I'll be careful. Will you? I won't follow it too far if it rises again. Far or not, you shouldn't follow it in the first place. All right, I won't. Will you promise? And the boy Mujae's father does promise, but from that day on he grows ever thinner, the words wasting away in his mouth, as though he has secretly started to follow his shadow. He blurts out things like, If you spot someone who looks just like you, it's your shadow, and once your shadow rises it's over for you, because shadows are very persistent, because you can't bear not to follow your shadow once it's risen. And then, looking like a ghost, he died.

He died?

He died.

Just like that.

Sometimes, people do die just like that.

Do you think my shadow would also be that dangerous?

I'm not sure, Mujae said, and I made an effort to keep up the pace, so as not to fall too far behind.

What would happen to me, Mujae, would I die just like that?

Mujae stopped in his tracks and turned to face me. Just don't follow your shadow, he said. You have to be careful not to follow, even if your shadow does rise.

⌁

WE CARRIED ON walking.

Now and then twigs snapped beneath our feet, sounding like wet bones breaking.

Mujae, I said, about sex. Do you think it's really that good?

It must be, don't you think?

Do you?

It must be, since some couples have so many children. I wonder.

Are you curious?

I just wonder.

Should we try it, when we make it out of here?

Do you think we really will make it out?

The woods won't go on forever.

I want to do it with someone I like.

Like someone, then.

Who?

Me.

Well.

I like someone.

Who?

You, Eungyo.

Don't joke around.

I'm not joking. I like you. I like you, Eungyo.

We pushed on and arrived at an animal shed. The sun had nearly set.

Look, Mujae said, and I turned to look in the direction he was pointing, and saw my shadow, which had become itself again, stretched out alongside Mujae's toward the woods from which we'd just emerged.

The sound of our approach sent a pair of deer skittering to a corner of the shed. We circled the shed, getting a whiff of the fur and excrement of herbivorous animals, and found ourselves in a small yard. A bulb hanging from the eaves of the

house illuminated the faces of a middle-aged couple, looking up at us from their meal. Since the
darkness was already thickening, they offered
to put us up for the night. We washed our faces,
put on the clothes they gave us, and ate a meal
of steamed rice wrapped in blanched mulberry
leaves. Night fell as we ate. The man, who introduced himself as "just a farmer," told us the name
of the village and its rough whereabouts. He called
it a village, but said that his was the only house
for several kilometers, and that in the morning
he would take us in his truck to a place where we
could catch a bus. Mujae and I thanked him. A fat
moth was stuttering around overhead, now beating
its wings against the bulb.

Mujae stood up and tucked his flat rice-bran
pillow under his arm.

See you in the morning, Eungyo.

After the two men had gone into the room next
door, the farmer's wife and I got ready to sleep.
The walls seemed very thin, as I could hear murmured voices coming from the other side. The
farmer's wife turned off the light, and the abrupt

darkness was like someone had cast a cloth over my eyes. I couldn't see a thing. My vision didn't improve even after some time had passed. I slowly brought my hand toward my face, but I still couldn't see a thing. The farmer's wife snored quietly. Whoo-whoo, owls cried outside.

Mujae, I called out quietly. There are owls here.

He must have fallen asleep already, or just not have heard me, as no answer came from beyond the wall.

The owls are crying.

I let the words hang in the air, lying quiet in the pitch-black darkness, distrusting even my own eyes.

A Whorl and a Whorl and What Isn't a Whorl

I SAID GOOD-BYE TO MUJAE at the subway station, where we each took different trains. By the time I got back to the area where I lived it was noon and the sun was blazing down as I dragged myself down the street. My stumpy shadow slanted to the right, bulging like a soft-boiled egg, its movements mimicking my own. When I thought about how it had risen now and then, the familiar shops and familiar alley didn't look familiar at all. I turned into the alley and heard the sound of television leaking out of a window. It sounded like a volleyball match, with a voice saying *spike*, very clearly enunciated, sounding more electronic than human. *Spike, spike, spike*, and I turned another corner. Fancy hearing a voice saying *spike*, I thought, then put my hands in my pocket, unable to recall what had come after. A sharp piece of paper pricked my finger. I pulled it out and saw that it was the wrapper from Mujae's gum. I bent it with my thumb, and it rustled like a shriveled ear.

I took down the pizza and fried chicken flyers that had been stuck to the door and stepped into the house. Inside it was dark, and seemed exactly how I'd left it even though I'd been gone a whole day. I took off my clothes, which smelled of soil, and went into the bathroom. I positioned myself beneath the naked bulb that dangled from the high ceiling, and looked down at my shadow. It looks a little bigger, I thought, and more thinned-out. I lifted my left foot up for a moment, then set it back down. I raised my right foot this time, put it down and lifted my left once more, then jumped up lightly so both feet were off the ground. The shadow spread out, a little thinner and wider, and definitely touched my feet when I put them down on the floor. I did a couple of jumps in my bare feet, examined the lightbulb, then turned on the hot water and washed my hair. Wiping the suds from my eyes, I thought to myself that even if my shadow had drawn me deep into the woods, so deep that I never returned, someone would still have stuck flyers on the door, and pizzas would still have been sold. I went back into the main room, lay down and pulled a blanket over myself. The weather was sultry, but my toes were cold. I wondered if this was because I had my feet pointing north, and shifted them a little to the east, my head a little to the west. But this didn't feel comfortable so I kept on shifting, again and again. I moved around so much I ended up back in my original position, but something still wasn't right. I felt as if my lower back had lifted up off the floor, the whole of me trembling like a compass needle. Falling in and out of sleep, haphazard thoughts flitted through my mind.

I worked at an electronics market, a ramshackle warren of tiny shops close to the heart of the city. The market had originally consisted of five separate buildings, labeled A, B, C, D and E, but had been altered and added to over a period of forty years so that it was now a single structure. You had to know where to look to spot the signs that it had ever been otherwise. The market was where I first met Mujae. I manned the customer desk and ran errands at Mr. Yeo's repair shop, while Mujae was an apprentice at a transformer workshop. One day I went down there with an old transformer that needed its copper wire replaced. There in that cramped space was Mujae, wearing wrist guards and an apron. Next to him, Mr. Gong was spinning the wheel with the copper wire twined around it. I held out the old transformer, needing both hands to lift its weight. Mujae took it casually in one, put it down on the table among all the copper wires, and made a note of the shop's name and phone number. The only remarkable thing about him was his beautiful handwriting. I'd seen him several times before, on my way in and out of the building or running errands to other workshops, but nothing had made those encounters stand out.

I nodded off, wondering whether I would see Mujae at work on Monday, since we'd said, See you on Monday. When I started awake, the sun was about to go down. The light of the setting sun filled the room. I realized that I'd left my packed lunch in the woods.

❧

MY SHADOW ROSE, I said, and Mr. Yeo blinked.

He was sitting on a stool, holding a probe connected to an oscilloscope. He furrowed his brow under his salt-and-pepper hair, blinked once, then twice, and asked,

So what did you do?

I followed it.

You followed it?

Just a little way.

You shouldn't have followed it.

I'm not going to any more.

That's right, Mr. Yeo said, touching the probe

to the circuit board and peering at the screen. The green line that had been streaming across the palm-sized monitor morphed into an undulating wave.

Those shadows, Mr. Yeo said, then stared intently at the monitor for some time. Whenever I assumed his thoughts had drifted he would reposition the probe, and when I thought he was engrossed in his task he suddenly came out with, Those shadows, you know. After a while more of this abstraction he finally looked up at me.

So how did you feel, when you were following the shadow?

Pretty good, I said. I couldn't help but follow it. Mr. Yeo nodded as if to say yes, that's how it is.

That's what's scary, you feel light somehow, carefree, if you surrender to the shadow's pulling at you, so you keep on following it, and that's when it strikes. People turn slow-witted when they're in that kind of daze, so it attacks when your wits are slowest of all, he said, and gently set the probe down on the worktable. Wait and see, it'll start growing now.

Growing bigger?

That's right.

And then what happens?

It becomes more dense. Gravity, or something.

Oh.

Don't worry too much. They say you can survive as long as you keep your eyes peeled, even if you're captured by a fox.

Isn't it a tiger?

What do you mean, a tiger?

The saying is that you can survive as long as you keep your eyes peeled, even if you're captured by a tiger.

A tiger, a fox, it's all the same, Mr. Yeo said, pushing a lamp with a tin hemisphere shade right up against the board. What I'm saying is, you need to keep your eyes peeled when what's in front of you has teeth.

❧

DO SHADOWS HAVE teeth?

Of course they do—they're attached to things that have teeth, aren't they?

And when they rise, they look a lot like the things themselves, since after all, these are shadows we're talking about, he said, and in the meantime our dosirak box lunches arrived, but Mr. Yeo set his aside, saying he didn't have an appetite. I ate my Young Master's Dosirak Box Lunch by myself, and went out to buy some ice flakes with syrup, at the request of Mr. Yeo who said he just wanted some ice. Mr. Yeo's repair shop was situated in Building B, which was second among the five buildings, Building A to the north being the first. Building B was also the most frequented of the five, though its air of dereliction was increasingly apparent, with one out of every eight shops having stood empty for months. On the ground floor, small appliances such as stoves, fans, and radios were sold, while the first to the third floors consisted of small shops barely managing to keep their heads above water, selling spare parts for various electronic devices, and household items such as brooms and mops. The fourth floor felt more isolated than the others; here, Mr. Yeo's repair shop shared the space with various storage facilities, jewelry appraisal shops, and radio labs, alongside shady-looking offices that claimed to be engaged in some form of research, though all that could be said for certain was that it was the kind which involved wiretapping.

As I descended the scuffed, worn-edged stairs I heard someone call my name. I turned around and saw Mujae at the top of the stairs, wearing wrist guards and a work apron.

You have a double crown, Eungyo. Two hair whorls, not one.

I know.

Have you seen them?

No.

You haven't?

I haven't had the chance, I said, and was about to ask whether a whorl wasn't something you had to make a special effort to see when Mujae chimed in with, That's too bad. Your whorls, Eungyo, have interesting shapes.

Whorls have shapes?

They do, Mujae said, arriving at the bottom of the stairs. He stood in front of me and looked into my eyes. It seemed weird to look away so I returned his gaze, then immediately realized that was just as weird, but by that point it was too late to do anything else so I just kept looking into his eyes. He was smiling, wordlessly.

Why are you smiling?

I'm not smiling.

Yes you are.

Have you had lunch?

No.

I blushed, flustered at having had the wrong answer jerked out of me. Mujae suggested that we go and get something to eat, and I followed him down the stairs. Once we reached the ground floor we left the building and crossed the parking lot, a dim, shadowy place even at the height of summer, then turned into an alley which coiled around the electronics market. We passed shops selling cables and all kinds of tools, then a row that specialized in repairing clocks and watches. A man standing outside his shop looked up from his newspaper as we walked past, fixing us with an intent stare. It felt awkward to just trail after Mujae in silence, so I wracked my brain for something to say and landed on the topic of Saturday's excursion.

I heard there were forty-six.

Forty-six what?

In the mountain. Mr. Yeo said that when they did a head count before coming back down the mountain, there were definitely forty-six people.

Really?

That's why they didn't realize that anyone was missing; because they counted exactly as many people as they'd started out with.

So two new people replaced the two who'd gone missing.

Is that what it means?

Do you think they were shadows?

I'm not sure.

They could have just miscounted, Mujae said, ducking in between two of the clock-and-watch shops. I thought we were turning down another alley, but when I followed him I saw it was a noodle restaurant. Once we'd sat down, Mujae took off his wrist guards, rolled them into a single ball and set it down on the table. A waiter brought us a kettle of steaming beef broth, and Mujae poured me a cup. The broth had a rich umami flavor. The cold noodles are really good, he said, and the beef rib soup. I said I'd have the beef rib soup, but when it came I wished I'd thought about the weather and ordered something cold. Mujae looked cool and comfortable as he ate his chilled noodles, whereas I had to keep wiping my forehead to stop the sweat dripping into my soup. Every time Mujae lowered his head to take a bite of his noodles, I saw his whorl neatly curling at the crown of his head.

About whorls, I began. If you asked ten people, How many of you have a whorl? how many do you think would raise their hand?

Hmm, Mujae said. Maybe all but one or two.

But probably all of them.

Probably, yes.

Then if you asked how many had taken a close look at it?

I'm not sure.

I always thought, Mujae, that a whorl was just a whorl—I never thought it could have a shape.

You mean a whorl that's a whorl, but not really a whorl?

What do you mean?

Try saying "whorl."

Whorl.

Whorl.

Whorl.

Whorl.

It's strange.

Whorl.

The more times I say the word "whorl," the more it seems like this whorl isn't the whorl we were talking about.

Yes, it seems that way, doesn't it? Whorl.

Whorl.

The thing about whorls, Mujae began, is that each one is unique. I read it in a book once that each person's whorl is a different shape.

Really?

We find it convenient to lump them all together as whorls, but from the whorl's point of view we're doing them quite a violence.

From the whorl's point of view?

A whorl might think, Hang on a minute, that guy called "Whorl" looks nothing like me! So that's why the more you say the word, the stranger it feels, because the truth comes out.

You think so?

Whorl.

Whorl.

Whorl.

It's confusing.

It is, isn't it?

Whorl, whorl, I repeated to myself, while absentmindedly examining a sliver of spring onion that had stuck to a corner of the table. What is a whorl, if it's a whorl that's a whorl but not really a whorl? This riddle had me more than a little puzzled. Mujae turned back to his noodles and cut the boiled egg in half with his chopsticks.

Do you like beef rib soup, Eungyo?

Yes, I do.

I prefer cold noodles myself.

Oh yes?

What other things do you like?

Well, this and that.

This and that what?

Just this and that.

I like people with straight collarbones.

You do, do you?

Yes, I do.

You like collarbones?

I like you, Eungyo.

But my collarbones aren't straight at all.

Yes, but with you it doesn't matter.

Is that so?

Want some egg?

Sure.

Mujae transferred one of the egg halves to my bowl, and popped the other half in his mouth. There was a mirror hanging on the far wall of the restaurant. I glanced at it and saw that my face was bright red. Mujae asked me why I was sweating so much. The soup's so hot, I said, and pressed a napkin to my sweaty forehead.

～

MR. YEO MIXED the sweet red beans into his shaved ice.

Do you like red beans, Eungyo?

Not really, I said. They're too sweet.

They're not that sweet, Mr. Yeo countered, then paused to eat a spoonful of the mixture. I wasn't a big fan of red beans either, when I was young. But now that I'm getting on in years I find myself craving it more and more—that, how can I put it, that subtle sweetness, that almost bitter bite they have. In the summer when it's really humid, just before the rains break, I dream of shaved ice with red beans, then in the winter when the cold gets into my bones, my mind turns to thick red bean porridge instead, with sticky rice on the side. Since we're on the subject, let me tell you about a friend of mine who had a real thing for red beans. He had a little factory that made electronics parts. He'd always regretted his lack of an education, so he sent his kids to the States, with his wife to look after them, and worked to support them. It must've cost him a great deal, to get them out there in the first place, and then the private school fees on top of that. And that's without taking the exchange rate into account. Your money goes ten times as far here than it does over there, and there was just no way he could earn enough to make up the difference. Still, he seemed to be giving it his best shot—doing odd jobs on the side, and scrimping wherever he could. He didn't even own a car, when he was, after all, a plant manager. Every time I saw him I asked him what the hell he was thinking living halfway around the world from his family, but he always laughed it off. He only visited them once a year, around Seollal or Chuseok, or twice a year at a push. The flights weren't exactly cheap, you know. Mr. Yeo broke off for a while, and crunched a few mouthfuls of ice flakes before resuming his story

One day, a little after Seollal, I was here in the workshop. A tube had been brought in a few days earlier, and I was wrestling with it till that hour because the problem wasn't that simple. Anyway, my friend pokes his head around the door, checking to see if I'm still here, and when he sees I am he comes right in. He'd brought us each a bowl of red bean porridge, though I can't think where would've been selling them at that time of night.

Let's eat, he said, so we did. I asked him if he'd spent Seollal with his family and he said yes he had. Everything's so big over there, he told me, the land itself is big and so are the houses they build on it, even my kids are big now, so big that they're not really kids any more. Jenny, my eldest, is fifteen; her friends came over to the house while I was there and I said, Hi, nice to meet you, and Jenny blushed and whisked them straight up to her room. Later, once her friends had all left, she asked him to please never talk to them again. Your English sounds weird, it's embarrassing, she said. My friend was taken aback at first, but then he burst out laughing. Later, though, he found he couldn't stop thinking about what she'd said. So he sat her down and gave her a good scolding, telling her she shouldn't treat her dad that way when he led such a difficult life. And this is what she said to him: You're the one who chose this life, not me, so there's no point acting the victim. You've no right to lecture me like this, you call yourself my dad but that's bullshit, you're barely ever here.

She said all that in English? I asked, and my friend just nodded like an idiot.

And you understood it all?

Well, he said, I got the gist.

I was really angry, genuinely quite upset, but I didn't want to let on so I just kept stuffing myself with the porridge. After a while I said, So, is that what you came to tell me? and my friend rubbed his face as though he was tired. No, that's not it, he said, it's just that lately, well, my shadow's been rising. He said that each night when he turned the lights off, his shadow would rise to the window. I live on the thirteenth floor, he said, but it still keeps rising.

At that, Mr. Yeo clamped his mouth tight shut. He sat there staring glumly into his bowl, then applied himself to the sweet snack as though hoping to stop his mouth with ice.

⌒

SO WHEN MY shadow rose, Mr. Yeo said.

By that time he had polished off the last of the shaved ice, which had melted into a pinkish puddle, fixed an amp that someone had brought in and sent it back to them.

It rose? I repeated, startled.

Mm, that's right. Mr. Yeo glanced over at me, nonchalant. My life hasn't exactly been plain sailing, so it was inevitable really—no big deal. I was at my front door when it happened, just putting on my shoes. I thought to myself, This is what you've been dreading, now it's finally happened, and I thought of my friend, the one I told you about, Eungyo. As I watched the shadow rise, it occurred to me that whoever made up the saying about your hair standing on end must have witnessed something like this. There was nothing I could do—I mean, it was a shadow. Once it had risen I could feel it pulling at me, and who knows what would've happened if I hadn't stood my ground? But I was more concerned by my family's odd reaction. The shadow didn't go far, just roamed around the house, and I wasn't sure whether my family genuinely couldn't see it, or whether they were simply pretending. This shadow would sit among us at mealtimes, you see. And my wife and kids never batted an eyelid, but at the same time they managed to avoid sitting near it, or touching it in any way. Whenever they passed each other one of the side dishes or a second helping of rice their arms never went too close to my shadow, and they even angled their heads slightly to the side so they could see each other round the shadow.

But shadows are visible, aren't they?

Of course they are. They were just pretending not to see what was clearly there, even when I pointed right at it and said, My shadow, that's my shadow. Like this, Mr Yoo said, and put his left thumb and forefinger together, as though to pinch the air. They'd just frown a little and glare as if they couldn't stand the sight of me. In a situation like that, wouldn't it be natural for me to think that they didn't care about me, that as far as they were concerned, I could follow my shadow and good riddance too? So then I started thinking, well, damn it, what's stopping me?

So you followed it?

Yes, but it wasn't easy. Because you've got your voice following too.

Your voice?

That's right, whispering in your ear the whole time: you mustn't, you mustn't. So anyway, I ended up turning back before I'd even gone ten miles. It was pathetic. I mean, what kind of idiot can't even follow their own shadow? I called myself all kinds of names. That night, the moon was so full and bright you could see its craters.

Mr. Yeo heaved a long sigh. I pictured him trudging wearily home with his shadow tacking along in his wake and the moon hanging bright in the night sky, its craters clearly defined.

It does still rise from time to time, but I tell myself it's no big deal. I can bear it as long as I tell myself that. It's not really true that it's no big deal, but the more I tell myself that it is the easier it becomes to believe it, and with time you really do end up convincing yourself. After all, shadows might rise, but they can also fall, can't they? It's risky, I know. Right now I can tell myself that it's no big deal, but there'll be a day when that doesn't work anymore, when it categorically is a big deal, and that'll be the end, Eungyo. My shadow will pull me after it, somewhere infinitely far away.

Mr. Yeo got a screwdriver out of a drawer and began to fiddle with the shell of the amp.

❧

THE REPAIR SHOP had two desks. Mr. Yeo used the one by the window, and I used the other. The metal top of Mr. Yeo's desk had started to buckle in the center from the weight of the amps, and neither of its three drawers would quite close properly, having been bent slightly out of shape. The long, shallow drawer that slid under the top of the desk contained dozens of screwdrivers, and the other two, arranged down the left side, held such an enormous variety of things that it would be difficult to give a precise inventory. Several years ago when I started working in the shop, my first task was to turn those two drawers upside down and rearrange their contents.

Some of the things that were in the drawers were: bits of wire, screws, screwdriver handles with the heads broken off, cassette tapes, labels, blister packs of pills, prescription slips, scrap paper, iron filings, electrical wires, bits of foil that had come off something or other, IC chips, broken pieces of circuit boards, punctured freezer bags, ballpoint pen refills, sewing needles, soldering lead, a wristwatch, bottle caps, leather strips, rubber bands, cords, wadded tissue, plastic film canisters filled with glue or textile conditioner, coffee powder, dust balls, squashed cigarette stubs, shriveled bugs like hard little nibs of corn, folded circuit diagrams, some desiccated material I found impossible to identify and, most bizarre of all, some bra hooks.

The bottommost drawer, which was also the deepest, contained coins in addition to those other things. Small change got tossed in there, and a thick layer of coins had accumulated at the bottom, which I discovered once I'd pulled out the rest of the clutter. I spread some newspaper out on the floor and spent half the day kneeling there, sorting through the coins. Mr. Yeo grumbled about the constant clinking, but didn't actually tell me to stop. Those who'd seen me counting the coins when they came to open up shop in the morning checked back in the afternoon to see if I was still at it. When I was finally done counting, just before sunset, the total came to one million, three hundred and fifty seven thousand, six hundred and forty won. I'd divided the coins by denomination as I counted, and now I put each pile into separate envclopes. They were so heavy I had to haul them to the bank in the cart we used for transporting amps. I had to stand in front of the counting machine for what felt like an age, pouring in the coins in dribs and drabs, waiting each time for the machine to register them. Finally, it confirmed the total amount: one million, three hundred and fifty seven thousand, six hundred and twenty won. I decided that we could afford an error of twenty won, and deposited the lot in Mr. Yeo's account. It had been years since he'd even glanced at the coins, and had no idea that the drawer had contained such a hoard.

The years passed and the drawer filled up again, but Mr. Yeo always insisted it be left as it was, that we ought to wait a while longer. That drawer was like a microcosm of the shop itself; both were dark as the inside of an iron whale's belly, and materially infinite. It looked as though a slightly higher dimension, let's say the 3.5th, had had a hole torn in the bottom of it through which everything had come crashing down. I spent my first year working there rearranging this and that. All the spare parts that Mr. Yeo left lying around got stored neatly away in drawers or cabinets, which I then labeled so we knew what was where. I divided the electrical wires, screws, and tools into separate groups. I devised a system for the amps, which had previously been stored in whatever order they'd come in, in teetering piles or clustered around the entrance to the shop. The shop was somewhat better organized once I'd finished, but still so crammed with stuff that first-time visitors would stand in the doorway with their mouth hanging open and ask how we ever managed to find anything.

Mr. Yeo had been there in that shop, fixing audio equipment, for more than thirty years. Given his skills he could have charged much more than he did, but his laid-back nature could sometimes be frustrating—fussy customers were quick to take offense, while rude ones received short shrift from him. In such cases, Mr. Yeo would put a little dot of paint inside the appliance or piece of equipment then, when the irate customer could find no one else to do the repairs, yet was too proud to admit defeat, so would get a friend to bring the selfsame item back to Mr. Yeo, or came themselves, all sunny smiles and feigned ignorance, he would wait until they'd left then open the lid, check the paint mark and gloat. And then he would fix the item and return it, also feigning ignorance.

The shop's window, whose glass bore a film of age and weather, looked out onto the sea of flat roofs which clustered around the noodle place where Mujae and I had eaten. Cats often slunk around on the sheets of corrugated iron. The shop's windowsill was almost rotten through; its black, damp wood crumbled like wet biscuit when I poked it with a finger. Sometimes, when a typhoon was raging, I'd have trouble falling asleep, picturing that old windowsill being sucked away by the fierce wind and whirled up into the air, ending up wedged somewhere in the iron rooftops.

⁓

HEY, IT'S ME, Yugon said as he barged into the repair shop. Mr. Yeo, will you lend me two thousand won?

What for? Mr. Yeo snapped back.

I plan on spending it, Yugon announced, placing a hand on his chest.

On what?

On a lottery ticket.

Oh, hell.

This time, the numbers are unmistakable.

Have your unmistakable numbers ever been otherwise?

This time, it's different.

How?

It's different in that the numbers are unmistakable.

Yugon perched on a stool in a corner of the shop and launched into one of his usual rambling speeches. My toes have been aching since I got up this morning, and the weather is always bound to be terrible when my toes ache like that, but there wasn't a cloud in the sky at first, so I lowered my guard, more fool me, because wouldn't you know it, by this afternoon I could feel the air growing heavy, and on my way here I saw a couple of umbrellas in a bucket outside a shop, I think they might be for sale; I think I left an umbrella here before, actually, I'm not sure if you've still got it, but in any case it must've come in handy sometime, so that's all fine by me; things getting left behind, that makes me think, you know, isn't it always a bit tricky when there's only one piece of rolled omelet left between two? Do you like rolled omelet? I do; he rattled this off as though he didn't care whether anyone was listening, constantly fiddling with the calculator on his lap, its plastic worn smooth and shiny from him always carrying it around.

It was hard to guess Yugon's age. He had a youngish face, but his shabby clothes looked strangely old-fashioned, yet surprisingly neat and tidy given how worn they were; then again, he didn't always wipe his nose when he needed to, and he looked smart yet slow at times, and tactless yet much too tactful at others. Yugon dropped by the repair shop once or twice a week. According to Mr. Yeo, these visits had been going on for more than a decade now, since Yugon was a boy, so I could only guess that he was between thirty and forty. He always had a wad of lottery tickets stuffed in his pocket, tied up with a rubber band. Whenever someone showed an interest in this bundle, he would feverishly tap out something on his calculator then tell the person to look at the numbers, saying that they were the result of such and such a calculation, and therefore it was unmistakable that they would be the next combination to come up in the lottery.

He would say,

You can't expect too much from people, but the lottery, that's a different matter,

or,

Will you lend me two thousand won?

and he would take the money if it was offered, but sometimes, even if his request had fallen on deaf ears, he would just carry on talking about this and that as if the money was neither here nor there, so it didn't seem that money was necessarily the reason he came. Sometimes he would show up after an absence of weeks, looking thin and pale, sit silently on the stool for a while, and then leave.

When I asked Mr. Yeo why he thought Yugon visited, Mr. Yeo said he came because he was lonely.

Lonely?

Some of the audio dealers who worked at the market asked Mr. Yeo why he gave money to a guy like that, but Mr. Yeo seemed more chary of them than of Yugon.

Is it okay if I have some water? Yugon asked. When I said it was he got quietly up from his seat and made his way deeper into the shop, maneuvering cautiously so as not to bump into any audio equipment. He stared at the rack on the top of the water dispenser and, after great hesitation, took a paper cup and half filled it with cold water. He tried to mix some hot water in, but realized that the safety button on the hot water valve meant that two hands were required. He stared down at the hand clutching the calculator, stumped; putting it down was clearly not an option. I knew it was bad manners, but I couldn't help staring as he floundered, juggling the calculator in one hand and the paper cup in the other before finally having the bright idea of tucking the calculator under his arm. Yugon gingerly extended a finger toward the safety button and succeeded in releasing the hot water. Finally, he transferred the calculator back to his left hand, and took a slow draft of his drink.

Hello, said Mujae. He stepped into the repair shop, greeted Mr. Yeo, set two newly fixed transformers down on the floor, then turned around and left. I hadn't seen him since our lunch together, that time when we'd sat there repeating whorl, whorl, so I stared at him despite myself, wondering if he was really going to leave just like that, when suddenly he turned around and beckoned. I raised my eyebrows to check if it was me he was beckoning. He nodded, and I followed him out of the shop. Mujae fished some small vivid globe from out of his apron pocket and held it out to me.

It was a flowerpot, round and russet as a ripe persimmon, with two thick seed leaves sprouting from it. It was made of plastic, smooth but not shiny. If you make a sound, he said, it moves.

The leaves, arched like a pair of eyebrows, bobbed up and down as if to verify this.

I took the flowerpot, which Mujae said he had bought on his way to work, and stared after him as he turned, tossing out a casual "see you later," and walked away. I went back in to the repair shop with the flowerpot balanced on my palm. Yugon, who in the meantime had returned to his spot by the entrance, regarded me quietly for a while.

Are you ill? he asked.

No.

Your face is flushed.

No it isn't. I placed the flowerpot on top of the cabinet, its leaves busily waggling up and down.

A Mouth That Eats a Mouth

IN AUGUST, THE RAINS CAME. It rained almost every day. It sccmcd as though the rain might never end. Whenever the sky cleared it was a matter of moments before it began to darken again, before fat raindrops would thicken into pouring sheets, then gradually thin out into a steady drizzle that would last all through the night. I found it stifling to sleep with a blanket, so on chill nights I just had the boiler on. One morning, I was in the middle of opening the fridge when I spotted a tiny green frog. I only just managed to avoid stepping on it.

It was about the size of a thumbnail, and its skin had a clear yellow tinge. I picked it up and sat it on my palm. Its tiny buttocks resembled a ripe cherry, and when I prodded them the frog puffed up its chin and shuffled around on my palm. I'd always thought that being cold-blooded meant frogs would feel cold to the touch, so I was surprised to find that wasn't the case. The frog's toes were clearly separated, each one small, thin, and see-through. I was taken aback to think that I might have crushed it. On my way to the bus stop I passed a clump of foxtails growing in a flowerbed and set the frog gently down on a leaf, which bent slightly under its weight. The frog remained motionless, angled down toward the ground, then abruptly hopped off the leaf and vanished into a thicket.

I got off the bus and crossed the parking lot, swinging my umbrella at my side. While I was waiting for the lift I spotted a notice on the wall and scanned it absentmindedly. The notice gave the date, time, and place of something called the "Tenants' Meeting regarding the Demolition of the Electronics Market." When Mr. Yeo arrived I asked him what it meant, and he said that there'd been talk of demolishing the market for a long time, but that nothing concrete had ever come of it.

I suggested that maybe they were holding a meeting because something was really going to happen this time, but Mr. Yeo just shrugged and said that in any case it was still a long way off. But a new notice appeared after the date of the meeting had passed, and banners were hung up, and everything started to feel very uncertain.

∽

HOW ABOUT WE go for some rice wine?

But it's Monday.

What does that matter? All this rain is chilling my stomach. Mujae walked on ahead, and I followed after. On our way we ran into Yugon. He was pacing up and down at the entrance to the market, clutching a paper bag containing a multiple-tap to his chest. From the way Mujae greeted him, it seemed that Yugon was also a frequent visitor at Mr. Gong's workshop.

I'm cold, Yugon said, his voice low and dejected. I don't have an umbrella, and my trousers are soaked.

Mujae suggested he come with us. We found a place near the bus station and sat down. Mujae and Yugon shared a kettle of warm rice wine, and I ordered a beer. The waiter brought us cucumbers and seaweed salad as snacks. There were roast blowfish fins floating in Mujae's and Yugon's cups.

Is this a tail?

I think so.

It looks like a big moth.

That makes it seem spooky.

It's kind of spooky in itself.

We drank in silence for a while, glancing from the liquid sloshing in our cups to the rain coming down outside. My ankle had gone to sleep so I tried to massage the feeling back into it, startled to find the skin icy cold. Lately, I'd been going home with wet ankles every day. I started to wonder about the frog. Was it still living in the flowerbed? Was it doing well there? The flowerbed was small, so the frog might have stayed there only briefly. Frogs can't really understand about flowerbeds, so it might have leaped out into the street and been trampled for real this time. If the frog really had died like that, was it my fault for putting it in the flowerbed? With these thoughts niggling away at me, I finished half my beer. The restaurant window was a haze of condensation. Mujae rubbed his finger over the glass, revealing raindrops clinging to the far side of the pane. The smell of vegetables being stir-fried in soy sauce drifted over from the kitchen. Yugon drank his rice wine slowly, setting the cup down after every sip so he could touch his calculator.

Do you know what a woodlouse is? he asked.

Of course, said Mujae.

A woodlouse, not a pill louse.

Is there a difference?

Oh yes, said Yugon. They're completely different organisms. He moved his finger over the table's surface, describing a tight little circle.

Pill lice can roll up into a ball like this, but woodlice can't. My room is infested with woodlice.

I've no idea where they come from, but when I look they're everywhere. I kill as many as I can, but there's just no getting rid of them.

Woodlice don't actually do any harm, Mujae offered. It's not like they suck your blood or anything.

Yugon straightened up and looked sternly at Mujae.

Whether something is harmful or not is a matter of personal standards. According to my own standards, woodlice are quite harmful enough. Even the dictionary says so, although the basic reason is their lack of aesthetic appeal. They're tiny, they have lots of legs, and they scuttle about. If a creature like that crawled into my ear while I'm asleep, wouldn't that count as harm?

Has that ever actually happened? I asked.

It's perfectly possible that it might, Yugon said, looking me straight in the eye. And that's not a chance I'm prepared to take. Even the thought is enough to make me shudder. A woodlouse crawling into my ear! That's why no one is allowed to tamper with the Bible in my room.

The Bible?

That's what I use to kill them. It's the ideal thickness, and always flies just as far as you need it to. Wall or ceiling, it gets the job done. You just open it up, aim, and throw.

By way of demonstration, Yugon brought his palms together at chest height then peeled them apart as if opening a book.

Of course, with the amount of woodlice I'm dealing with, both the Bible and the walls get dirty pretty quick. The Bible's all right because it's got so many pages, but every now and then I have to put up new wallpaper.

I see.

It's a terrible nuisance.

A group of men in suits barged into the restaurant and proceeded to kick up a fuss. They stayed standing just inside the door for an inordinate amount of time, shaking their umbrellas dry and exclaiming about the weather, arguing loudly over the relative merits of one table over another, before they all finally piled into one that was tucked away in a corner. As they jostled past our table, smelling of rain-soaked fabric, a stiff bag threatened to brush against me. I flinched away, hunching my shoulders in an effort to make myself smaller, and at that moment Mujae asked me how my shadow was doing these days.

My shadow? I echoed, momentarily surprised. It's okay, nothing special. At least, it's shown no signs of rising again.

Even if it does, Mujae told me, you mustn't follow it, Eungyo.

I won't, I said, and was just bringing my cup to my mouth when my eyes met those of Yugon, who was gazing blankly in my direction.

Your shadow rose?

Yeah, it did.

It did, huh. Yugon pushed his cup slightly forward. Mine rises too, from time to time.

Is he suggesting a toast? I wondered, and touched my cup to his, but this seemed to startle him, so I must have been mistaken. He fiddled with his cup, frowning slightly, then pulled it back as if to hide it with his hands.

BUT ANYWAY, YUGON said. Do you really think wood-lice don't bite? They have mouths, don't they? What else would their mouths be for? If something has a mouth, it stands to reason that it bites.

⌒

I WAS TWELVE when my father died. He was working on the construction site of an apartment building. The anchor of a tower crane fell on him from a height of thirty meters. His death was such a certainty that the anchor wasn't removed until three full hours later. My mother still insisted on seeing the body, on taking a last look at his mangled remains while the rest of us were sitting in the funeral hall. I sat with my father's sisters, who were all dressed in mourning clothes. This was over ten years ago, but certain details are still vivid in my mind. How the hall's wooden floor was so cold that I shivered when I first stepped onto it; how my mother later reappeared and sat down beside us, strangely calm, then gently tugged at my clothes;

that there were small beads of sweat on the nape of her neck, which I saw when she leaned in to talk to me; that her mourning clothes smelled of burnt almonds; that a string fastening her skirt had come undone and was dangling below her breasts; her voice as she said, That's not your father, they've hidden him away somewhere and put a pig in his place; how I instantly pictured a bloodied pig lying on a cold metal bed.

I'd never seen one of those beds before, worn and scuffed from all the corpses it had borne, polished to a shine by the cloth used to wrap them. I still wonder how I could have pictured it so clearly without ever having seen one, its planes and curves, the way it would feel to touch.

A lot of people came to pay their respects, including a steady stream of Catholics. I remember how the prayers they recited continued like a round, almost like a Buddhist chant. On the day of the coffin rites, people carried lit candles as they filed into the room where my father lay. He'd already been clothed in hemp, his hands and face so thickly swaddled they were merely featureless balls. There were so many people squeezing into the room that I couldn't get close enough to see my father. I couldn't tell how many of them had actually known him, but most of their faces were unfamiliar to me, and I thought that many must be seeking some kind of inspiration from an unfortunate corpse whom they'd never known in life. All I could see from where I was standing was my mother's profile, hovering above the arm of a woman's black jacket that gave off a sharp smell of sweat. My mother's relatives were propping her up, and the candle she was clutching with both hands was tilted at such an angle that I couldn't take my eyes off it, worried that the flame would set fire to the coffin, though they were far too far apart for that to be a genuine possibility.

After the funeral my mother spent some time in the hospital, and when she came home she was carrying a shadow on her back. The shadow was quite large by then, and was so dark it defied description. It was so tightly attached to her back that you couldn't tell who was clinging to who. My aunt had looked after me while my mother was in the hospital, and when she saw my mother's shadow she decided she ought to stay on. The two of us tried everything we could think of, throwing handfuls of red beans at the shadow, shouting, trying to sweep it off with a broom, but it was no use, and though the shadow repeated, I'm scared, I'm scared, its voice was empty of any fear. My mother stayed cooped up in her room with the shadow, refusing to wash or eat properly.

My aunt and I decided to give the house a good clean-out, thinking that it might do us all some good to get some fresh air circulating. Right at the back of the fridge, behind the tubs of kimchi and other side dishes, I found a metal container the size of a lunchbox. I didn't know how long it had been there, but it was incredibly cold. Inside, I found several lipsticks. They were pink, red, and orange, each covered with beads of water or a mold-like film. I showed the box to my aunt, she told me to throw it away, and I did. After that, I promptly forgot that there had ever been such a box.

So when, out of the blue, my mother asked for her metal box, my aunt and I couldn't immediately recall what she was talking about. When my mother began to describe the lipsticks inside, I was sure that it was that box, and told her that I'd thrown it away a few days ago. Bring it back, my mother said. My aunt explained that she was the one who'd told me to throw it away, but my mother's gaze continued to bore into me. Bring it back, she said, still with the shadow clinging to her, and her eyes glinted.

Bring it back, my mother said, and her shadow said Bring it back.

Bring it back, her shadow said, and my mother said Bring it back.

As she and her shadow took turns to speak the words, my mother's voice grew gradually weaker until only her shadow was audible, a round shape looming over her shoulder that could almost have been a head. The shadow was opening and closing something that might be called a mouth, a little hole set into its darkness, and soon it was merely producing strange sounds, like *mimi* or *gaga*, as if vocalization itself was the aim. My aunt and I apologized profusely, explaining that the box would have been taken away several days ago and therefore could not be brought back. In the end we prostrated ourselves in front of my mother, begging for forgiveness, but no forgiveness came. Her shadow was darker than ever, now covering every part of her body, but she didn't try to shrug it off, as if she wasn't aware of it or simply didn't care. Now and then she opened her mouth and repeated after the shadow, Mimi, gaga. I watched her mouth hanging slack, saw her shadow slipping furtively in and out, turning her tongue black. I don't know how long I stood there watching it. In the end, my aunt snapped me out of it. Your shadow, she said, her voice wavering, and I turned my head and saw it: stretched out toward the front door, curling at the edges like peeling wallpaper and fluttering in the still air.

❧

THAT WAS THE first time, Yugon said, those last words drowned out by the party of businessmen beginning to pound their fists on their tabletop. One of the five got to his feet, holding a large glass of beer.

The loosened knot of his tie had slid down to his shirt's third button, and the veins on his wrist were bulging from the weight of the glass. He hefted the glass to his mouth and downed the beer in great gulps, with his left hand pressed to his stomach. The rest of his party beat the table with their eight fists, slowly at first, then faster and faster, until at last he had drained the glass, or near enough, and thudded it down onto the table. Mujae, Yugon, and I watched in silence.

The restaurant's employees were watching as well, looking bored, their elbows on the counter.

I should head back.

I turned back to our table and saw Yugon stand up from his seat, clutching his paper bag.

Have another drink, Mujae encouraged him, but Yugon shook his head.

I shouldn't have told that story, he said, I feel like this place is swarming with shadows now. He stepped out into the rain, refusing our proffered umbrellas, and once we'd seen him off the two of us went back inside. There was a blowfish fin, still wet, in Yugon's abandoned cup.

Mujae didn't finish the last bit of his wine, saying it tasted fishy now it had gone cold. The rain had turned into a light drizzle, so thin that you could only make it out in the haloes of light around the streetlamps. We stood under the restaurant awning to put our umbrellas up, then set off toward the subway station. I trudged along the puddle-pocked road, trying to hold my umbrella up properly with my limp hands, feeling the alcohol taking effect. My shadow spread out under the light of the streetlamps, from those shop fronts that stayed open into the small hours. Though overlapped, my shadow and the shadow of the umbrella slightly differed in their density. I looked down at my feet as I walked, thinking, Shadows don't disappear easily even at night. Mujae offered a penny for my thoughts.

It's nothing, I said. I'm just feeling a bit down, because I can't really think of anything fun to do.

How about we sit there for a bit, Mujae said, pointing to a wisteria gazebo in front of a large building, probably intended for its employees to eat their lunch on fine days, or take a cigarette break.

Won't the benches be too wet to sit on? To myself, I thought, But more importantly, will it be fun to sit there? Mujae walked over to check, then called me over.

This one is okay, he said, and when I sat down it wasn't as damp as I'd expected. Mujae sat down next to me, though he left a little space between us. We were side by side under the wisteria, holding our umbrellas. Wet flowers were scattered here and there over the brick-paved ground where the rain could not soak away. Every now and then, a raindrop would fall from the wisteria roof and plunk onto the taut umbrella material. As I sat there under my umbrella and listened to that sound, my mood did seem to lift a little, though I still wasn't exactly having fun.

Should we sing? Mujae suggested. Which song do you like, Eungyo?

I like Chilgapsan.

I can't sing that one.

You don't know it?

I do, but I can't sing it.

How come?

I get choked up at "a patch of beans."

Really?

It says that a woman weeding a patch of beans is weeping so hard the tears soak her hemp sleeves, that she plants a tear in each beanstalk as she moves through the patch, that she gets married and moves far away, leaving her mother all alone on a mountain ridge, with only the birdsong for company . . .

I see. We gazed wordlessly out at the nighttime street. Each time a car drove by, its headlamps shed yellow light onto the falling rain.

I heard, said Mujae, that if a couple boil wisteria leaves and drink the water together, their relationship will be healed.

Oh?

If our relationship ever gets damaged, shall we boil some wisteria leaves?

Well, I said, flustered, but we're not a couple. Mujae smiled from ear to ear. I cleared my throat. I don't know about relationships, Mujae, but it's nice sitting here like this, warm inside from the rice wine.

Yeah.

It's just, you know. Nice.

We lapsed into silence and sat there, watching the night.

~

FOR SEVERAL WEEKS after that, Mujae and I didn't spend any time together. At least, not just the two of us, like we had that day. Appliances always came flooding into the repair shop around the end of the rainy season. I had no call to go down to Mr. Gong's workshop, as only a handful of cases had a problem with the transformer. Mujae did visit the repair shop a couple of times, but he, too, must have been busy with work, as he rushed back down each time as soon as his errand was over. When, on occasion, I happened to be passing by the workshop, there was only Mr. Gong, spinning the wheel or smoking a cigarette.

One day Yugon came by and announced that he had a cold, then, after rambling on about this and that, gave me five chocolate bars in return for the rice wine.

Blackout

THE RAINS STOPPED, BUT THE heat wave continued. The thick white clouds against the sky's clear blue were pleasing to the eye, but the sweltering heat was unbearable. Even the briefest venture out into the sun made me break into a sweat, and when the sweat dried my forehead felt unpleasantly chilled. On Sunday, I took my bicycle out for the first time in a while, down to the river to get some fresh air, then headed to the house where my father lived. I cycled slowly at first, muscles relaxed, but then began to push down hard on the pedals. After cycling the distance of three bus stops, I arrived at the house. The outer wall had been recently demolished, so the heap of broken bricks hadn't yet been cleared away, and the cluttered yard was open to view. I secured my bicycle to the water pipe and unlocked the front door. It's me, I called out, but there was no answer. My father wasn't home. I couldn't spot his fishing gear, so I guessed that was where he'd gone.

I flung open all the windows and cleaned the house from top to bottom, though there wasn't really much that needed doing. Light streamed through the south-facing windows and puddled onto the hall's wooden floor. Dust motes swirled up as I plied the broom, and dust flew up in a swirl. In the bathroom I discovered three large rubber tubs, each full of fish. One held carp, another held loach, and in the third, much less densely packed than the others, were several catfish. The sight was a familiar one to me, and had been since early childhood. I crouched down and peered into the tubs. Some of the carp were already floating on the water, pale silvery bellies exposed. One small fish was lying on the tile floor. Out of the water, its glassy eyes had filmed over and its scales had lost their sheen. I jiggled on my haunches so my legs wouldn't get numb, then cautiously shifted the tub of loach. I watched quietly as a thin stream of bubbles appeared, then slipped my hand just below the surface. The water felt oddly slippery, clinging to my skin.

I'd never really let on, but I'd always hated that my father kept the catch from his fishing trips in our bathroom, a stock that was replenished every few days. The smell that permeated the house, the scales that stuck to my skin whenever I had to use the sink, the sound of the fish slowly suffocating, which frequently kept me awake at night.

A few times I'd hinted at my discomfort by asking who was going to eat all this fish, but I never did get any answer.

That was the father I grew up under.

You could say he made an indifferent parent, or simply that he was taciturn by nature—he always packed my lunch for school, for instance, but the only side dish I ever got was pickled radish from the store. We never talked much. When I was little, every time the holiday season came around and the family got together his sisters would be on at him to remarry, but my father never let himself be drawn into these discussions, and nothing ever came of their efforts. My mother left home when I was very young, so I never knew much about her. That she used to work at a high-end Korean restaurant; that my father's family got the shock of their lives when he showed up with her one day; that they lived together without a wedding ceremony; that she was much too pretty, much too young, with breasts that were much too large; that she came to a bad end just as my aunts had predicted, running away with another man; this was all gleaned from their hushed conversations, or read between the lines of pointed remarks. My own memories were nothing more than a handful of vague fragments. The texture of a calico skirt, its hem balled in my tiny fist; the scent of chewing gum; slender arms that lifted me up onto the bus, a grip that was surprisingly firm. Before she left, my mother emptied out a cardboard case of face powder and filled it with bright hair bands. Their elastic was decorated with plastic strawberries, carrots and watermelons, purple flowers, all of which I lost long ago, along with the case itself.

When I'd finished sweeping and went to close the front door, I noticed something black lying on the porch steps.

It was a cicada. It was a thick, stumpy thing, and one of its wings was torn at the tip. I leaned closer, wondering if it was dead, and it lifted its square head as if daring me to touch it.

～

IT WAS MY father who got me the job at Mr. Yeo's repair shop, through a loose thread of acquaintances. I left school when I was seventeen. I went through some things—bullying—that couldn't simply be dismissed as the usual kids' stuff. For a while I tried to bear up under it, thinking that the bullies would have to get bored someday, but everything changed when I ran into a classmate outside of school. We were walking down the same side of the street, heading in opposite directions. She'd always been one of the most aggressive, so I was sure she wouldn't let this opportunity slide. I kept walking, sick with nerves but holding my head up, but she passed by me without so much as slowing her step, head down as though embarrassed. I was confused, but simply took it as a stroke of luck and carried on down the street. The next day, though, seeing her back to her usual tricks, surrounded by her usual gang, something inside me just broke. I could no longer see the point of affecting indifference in the face of such a strange, meaningless malice, or of trying to fit in with the group. I picked up my bag and walked out of the school. Idiots, idiots, all the way home the word ran through my head, and all evening I carried on repeating it to myself, and that was the last day I attended school. My father saw, of course, that I didn't go off to school when it was time, but he never said anything about it. Roughly a month went by in this way, and in the end it was me who broke the silence, announcing that I'd quit school, to which all he said was, All right.

All right, was all he said when I told him I wanted to work, and again when I walked out of our house a month later, having already rented a room nearby and had my belongings sent ahead of me.

From somewhere in the middle distance a group of cicadas broke into a high chorus, and a few moments later a low buzz could be heard from the stairs, a feeble attempt at emulation.

I found a squash in the fridge and made a batch of soup, enough for three or four meals. I ate a bowlful myself, with rice and kimchi on the side, there at my father's house, though without my father there. Through the window I'd flung open I could see a middle-aged woman with a cloth tied around her head, laboring up a slope that led to the nearest mineral spring, empty plastic bottles bumping together in her handcart. The shrill cry of the cicadas fell from somewhere high up and far away. The cicada on the stairs, meanwhile, only had the energy for a low, fitful buzzing, that petered out after a minute or so.

I washed and stacked the dishes before leaving the house. The cicada, I noticed, was now lying on its back.

Good-bye, I said, and closed the door behind me.

❧

WE HAD A visit from Mr. Park, who ran a repair shop in Building A, about the same size as Mr. Yeo's. Unloading two vacuum tube amplifiers from his cart, he asked for Mr. Yeo's help, saying he'd been working on them for several days and still hadn't cracked the problem. While the two men talked, examining the amps together, I offered one of our rather shabby chairs to Mr. Park's companion. He was an elderly man, neatly turned-out and with an air of respectability. He didn't turn his nose up at the seat but accepted it graciously, and maintained an excellent posture as he watched the two repairmen. Mr. Yeo set the amps to one side and asked Mr. Park about the intended demolition of Building A, which was apparently becoming more concrete by the day. The latest proposal included an offer to pay all moving expenses, even for those whose businesses were unlicensed, and that any who wished to would be able to reestablish their shop in the temporary market, whose construction was nearing completion, where, moreover, they would only be charged a basic maintenance fee for the first few months. This all seemed reasonable enough at first glance, but Mr. Yeo was skeptical, saying that the other traders had been asking where this so-called temporary market was. Are you planning to move there? asked Mr. Yeo, and Mr. Park said that he was.

What do they have there?

Nothing much.

So why are you going?

Things will get better.

The old man who had come with Mr. Park leaned toward me and asked, Have you seen the old woman who was outside?

Was there an old woman? I wondered, and told him I hadn't, and Mr. Park turned around and said, Mother's at home, Father. Mr. Park introduced the old man to the startled Mr. Yeo, explaining that his father had recently had a big chunk of his shadow ripped off, more than half in fact, and had been acting oddly ever since, not constantly but periodically, so Mr. Park tried not to leave him at home too often, and hoped that getting him out and about might give him some of his old energy back and make up for his lost shadow. Now that I knew to look, the shadow around the old man's feet was indeed unusually faint. Mr. Yeo said hello to him and the old man said hello back, smiling in a courteous and entirely normal manner, but a moment later he got up from his seat and wandered out of the shop, casting around for something or other, and Mr. Park had to go and fetch him back, holding him firmly by the hand. Mother's at home, Father, Mr. Park said, and the old man said, No, it's not the old woman I'm looking for, it's my shadow, but he followed Mr. Park back inside without any fuss, sat down in his chair and stayed there, perfectly composed, as if he'd completely forgotten that he'd tried to wander off. Mr. Park and Mr. Yeo returned to discussing the problem of the amps. Now and then I would catch the elder Mr. Park's eye, and each time that happened he would ask the same question. He talked about other things too, like yesterday's weather or his favorite model of vintage amp, but then he would ask me where the old woman was, the one he claimed to have spotted just moments ago, and each time Mr. Park turned around and said, She's at home.

We saw the old man to the door when Mr. Park left, watching him meekly consent to being led by the hand, and then I asked Mr. Yeo if we, too, would move to the temporary market, when it was Building B's turn to be knocked down.

Mr. Yeo shook his head.

It's not free, you know.

Where will we go, then?

To Building C, Mr. Yeo said.

Will there be enough space?

He scratched his head and said there should be plenty, since Building B was already so empty; though that emptiness was itself a problem, he said, he couldn't just up sticks and abandon three decades' worth of business connections.

That day, I ran into Mujae while I was down on the ground floor. I heard someone call my name, turned around and saw him there, standing on the other side of the parking lot. He looked tired, and the box he was carrying needed both arms to heft it. He crossed the parking lot, looking both ways, and when he reached me he said, It's been a while.

It has.

Can I call you?

Please do.

He asked for my phone number and I was going to write it down for him, but neither of us had a pen. I recited the number twice and asked him if he thought he could remember it.

I'll remember it. I'll call you, Mujae said as he left, and I stood there looking after him for a while.

When several days had passed with no phone call, I fell into a sulk. Fine, I thought, if that's how it is.

❧

I WAS WASHING up a mug when the lights snapped off.

The fridge motor whirred to a stop. The street lights looked to be out as well. It was quiet. I

wanted to have my hands free, so I put the mug
down on a surface I guessed was the shelf. But
my guess must have been wrong, as the mug fell
to the floor with a deafening crash. I stood there
in daze. I knew the shards were scattered over
the floor, but I could barely see and didn't know
how to move without cutting myself. It occurred
to me to turn on the gas range, but the light of
its blue flame wasn't enough to see the floor by.
I wondered if there were any candles somewhere,
but I had no memory of ever buying such things.
Feeling utterly useless, I turned off the gas. My
groping fingers managed to seize on a dish rag,
which I used to sweep the spot in front of my feet
as I gingerly inched my way forward. My calves
throbbed, but I kept on shuffling until I reached
the door to my bedroom. I crumpled to my knees
and lay face down, with my head on the raised sill.
I no longer wanted to move. The heel of my right
foot stung, probably impaled with a shard of glass,
and I seemed to have injured my right leg too. I
touched my hand to my calf and felt something
slippery, though I couldn't tell if it was blood or

sweat. I pressed down on it where it throbbed. I couldn't lift my head, because I felt a chill along my spine as if my shadow were about to rise, taking advantage of my vulnerability as I lay wounded in the darkness. When I thought that the shadow might have already risen and merged with that larger darkness, seeping into a corner somewhere, the darkness seemed to grow even darker, and I felt afraid. This fear was followed by a surge of anger, anger at myself for not stocking a single candle, and when that subsided I began to cry because I had an itch but couldn't find the spot to scratch it, which was annoying, and then I stopped crying, and then I became even more depressed.

With my nose kissing the sill, I stared at a slightly darker spot which I assumed was a knot in the wood, and breathed in the smell of it, which seemed both wet and dry. I might as well be dark, I thought. If I were dark myself then I wouldn't be hemmed in by the darkness around me, or fear that darkness, would I? What if I became dark and indifferent? If that happened, what would I be? What name could I give it? Oh, I don't know, I don't know, I should just become dark so I don't have to think about it, and while I was thinking this I opened my eyes, and then the phone rang. I moved toward the sound and groped around on the low shelf until my hand closed around the receiver. I tugged it down, knocking a shower of small objects to the floor, and sank back onto the door sill, my left cheekbone pressed against its wood. I put the receiver to my right ear and found that it was Mujae calling. Eungyo, he said, his voice slightly cracked, and he coughed. Is your power out, too?

Yeah.

It's dark here, too, he said, then was silent for a while. Why are you crying? Mujae asked.

I'm not crying.

You are.

Leave me alone.

Are you scared?

Yeah.

You're an idiot.

I'm not an idiot.

Yes you are, Mujae said, and sighed.

Mujae, I said.

Yeah, he said.

Don't hang up.

I'm not going to.

You can call me an idiot, but don't hang up, I said, and listened to the sound that came from his end.

⌣

HOW ABOUT WE sing, Eungyo?

You sing to me.

Which song?

Footprints.

Remind me how that one goes?

Footprints in the white snow. Footprints, side by side with paw prints. Who, who left at the break of day?

I can't sing that song.

How come?

I'm choking up.

This one makes you choke up, too?

It says that someone left at the break of day, with only a dog as a companion, and nothing but footprints remain.

You don't have to sing it, then.

I don't, right?

Although you kind of did already.

I'll sing something else.

Tell me a story instead.

What kind of a story?

A story about the boy Mujae.

How far did we get?

The boy's father died. What happened after that?

The boy went on living.

Okay.

The boy's name was Mujae, said Mujae, and he was quiet for a while, and then he said, How about we leave it there?

Why?

A story like that is too bizarre for a night like this.

What's so bizarre about it?

The boy's father dies, leaving his debts behind, and the boy grows up, struggling to pay off those debts.

Is that what happens?

The boy goes into debt to pay that debt, and gets into other debts to pay the interest on the debt, and everything he earns gets sucked up by the debt, so he has to go into more and more debt just to pay for rent and food.

. . .

You tell me a story, Eungyo. One that isn't too bizarre.

A story about Omusa, then.

Omusa?

Don't you know Omusa, Mujae?

No, I don't.

Omusa is a shop where an old man sells lightbulbs. Not the ordinary lightbulbs people use in their homes, but the tiny bulbs used in things like flashlights and microwaves, the kind that cost ten, fifty, a hundred won apiece. When you buy a pack of bulbs at Omusa you always come away with one extra. When you buy a pack of twenty, you get it home and find that it contains twenty-one, when you buy forty, you find forty-one, when you buy fifty, you find fifty-one, when you buy a hundred, you find a hundred and one.

Could it be that the owner makes a mistake when he counts them?

That's what I thought, but when I kept finding that extra bulb, no matter what size of pack I'd bought, and always just one, I thought that it couldn't be a coincidence. I asked the old man about it the next time I went to Omusa, and he looked up from the bulbs he was counting but didn't say anything. I was nervous, thinking that maybe I shouldn't have mentioned it, but when I looked more closely I saw that his lips were twitching, as though he was working himself up to speak. After a while, he said that he always packs an extra bulb in case one breaks in transit, or one is defective, since he doesn't want his customers to have to come all the way back to his shop. When I heard that I felt, I don't know, touched, because, well, you know "buy one get one free"? Do you ever get those offers, Mujae, at the big discount stores?

Sometimes.

When you buy one thing and they give you another of the same, you feel like you've gained something, but somehow, you don't feel that they did it out of any genuine consideration for you.

That's true, now I think about it.

But with Omusa I liked how it felt that I was being given a precious gift, even though it's such a small, cheap thing.

I see.

Mujae.

Yeah?

Now go on with the story.

I'd rather sing.

Sing me a song, then.

Footprints on the white snow . . .

Even though he'd said it made him choke up, he sang the song to the end, finishing with, Footprints on a lonely mountain path.

One more time, I said, and he didn't protest, just sang to me calmly down the phone, Footprints on the white snow.

Omusa

I ONCE GOT LOST WHILE running an errand at the market.

Without realizing it, I'd passed from Building B into Building A. I'd worked in the market for years but had somehow strayed from my usual route, finding myself utterly lost within a structure that looked familiar but was subtly different. I went up to the thirteenth floor to get my bearings. Looking down from the rooftop with the wind in my face, I could see the five buildings, from A to E, lined up in the heart of the city like a marker pointing toward the river. They looked like five enormous buses that had had their wheels removed, their bellies now dragging on the ground. They were each eight stories high, except for Building A, which was taller. I'd never gone further than Building C, and even that had only been a one-time errand. Clinging to the barbed-wire fence, I looked down at the rooftop of Building B. There was a man there smoking, looking down over the edge just like I was, studying the city streets.

I came down once I'd figured out generally where I was, but by then I had no chance of finding the place whose location Mr. Yeo had only told me in words. All I could do was return to Building B and get a map from Mr. Yeo. He said I ought to go straight down to the ground floor without crossing over into Building A, although he didn't know where and how I'd gotten lost. Finally, after following the map Mr. Yeo had sketched out for me, a vague set of lines and curves on the back of a crumpled receipt, I managed to find the place I'd been sent to.

That place was Omusa.

OMUSA WAS A shop that sold lightbulbs.

It wasn't the kind of place you'd notice as a casual passerby, but one you could only find if you were looking for it.

Let's pay a visit to Omusa.

When you alight in front of the cinema, having traveled there by subway or bus, your hundred-meter walk to the electronics market takes you past stalls displaying dried-up lizards, alarm clocks, synthetic leather belts, batteries, shoes, and hats, before bringing you to the northern corner of Building A. When you turn right at the lighting shop that has a mirror fixed to a pillar outside, you enter the ground floor of the market, which functions as a parking lot, and there you encounter the old woman with bobbed gray hair who has constructed a lean-to for herself by stringing flattened cardboard boxes between the staircase and the ground, like a folding screen; you'll invariably find her sitting on the ground a couple of meters from her makeshift home, watching the road as if waiting for someone. I once saw a passerby offer her a custard bun; she regarded the pastry with an expression of faint puzzlement, reached out and took it as if it were some bizarre, potentially dangerous creature, tucked it between her knees and chest and turned her gaze firmly back to the road. You'll walk past her, keeping the parking lot on your left and the shops selling lighting or tools on your right, turn into the first alley on the right and come across a blank-faced, middle-aged woman who has been doling out blood sausage in the same spot for twenty years, her "stall" no more than a single oil drum. Further down the alley there'll be glass cases containing pocket watches, copper alarm clocks, and tarnished silver spoons, with elderly men parked in front of them, dozing off in front of their wares. There'll be a handful of tiny shops as well, one selling cigarettes, drinks, and boiled eggs, one selling spare parts, and one where you can get old radios repaired, each one so cramped that there is only room for a standing counter. You'll turn down a still narrower alley, or more precisely, a dark passage you'll initially mistake for a gap between two buildings, you'll see a shack which dishes up rice and kimchi as a meager takeaway lunch—across from it is Omusa. It's a dingy old place that looks straight out of the nineteen-seventies. Its walls are lined with bundles of little yellow and blue bulbs, yet there is no bulb to light up the shop itself.

Jam-packed.

If the word was included in a picture dictionary, the entry would probably be illustrated by a scene like that of Omusa's interior.

It's jam-packed, I thought, and could think of no other word to describe it, so jam-packed was this shop I was seeing for the first time.

The old man who works there is in his seventies, with a full head of hair though it has long since turned gray. He has a wooden chair and a wooden desk, where he sits with his back to a shelf crammed full of corrugated cardboard boxes. He sits there lost in thought, gazing absentmindedly at something or other, until a customer comes in and asks for a certain type of bulb. Then, without hurrying, but without dithering either, he slowly pushes his chair back and gets to his feet, gropes along the shelf until he gets to the right section, slides one of the boxes out as though removing a brick from a wall, sets it down on the desk and flips back the worn-out lid, then shuffles over to a different shelf to fetch a small plastic pouch which he opens with care, taking his time, then slips his right hand into the cardboard box and grabs a handful of fingernail-sized bulbs which he drops one by one into the plastic pouch, its round opening ready to receive, like putting rice puffs into the mouths of an eager baby sparrow, as I happened to hear another customer remark one time when I was waiting my turn.

Even if you rushed over to Omusa on urgent business and hurriedly told the old man what you needed, time flowed at his pace only, so customers would end up having to kill time by ogling Omusa's jam-packed interior or snacking on some boiled eggs from the shop next door. The old man, though slow, moved with great concentration, and this measured economy of his kept the customers from trying to rush him. Those who were particularly impatient might grumble a little, but they never asked him to hurry up, and they never took their business elsewhere. The boxes at Omusa had been there for so long, they contained bulbs that could no longer be found anywhere else. If you looked closely enough you could see that some of the boxes had little pen marks on them, but the majority were unmarked, yet somehow the old man at Omusa was never thrown; no matter what kind of bulb you asked for, his slow steps would take him in a direct line to the correct section of shelf.

What will happen to all the bulbs when the old man dies? Without him, who will possibly manage to fathom out which bulbs are where? Won't whoever takes over end up chucking out rare bulbs just because they're old? Each time I visited Omusa such thoughts would leave me feeling at a loss, but some of our own customers voiced similar thoughts about the repair shop and Mr. Yeo, and every time they did I was reminded of the repair shop's own history.

One day I went down to buy some bulbs and both the old man and the shelves were gone.

Only the dark walls remained, enclosing an empty space.

He's passed away, I thought.

I came back to the repair shop and broke the news, which left Mr. Yeo looking troubled for some time after. The bulb I'd wanted to buy was no longer being manufactured, so the appliance that required it had to be sent back as it was, without being repaired. After those bulbs stopped being made, there was a notable increase in the number of repairs that required them, and Mr. Yeo and I often remarked how strange it was that you always notice something more when it's gone, how sad it all was.

⌒

SUMMER WAS SLIDING into autumn when I found Omusa again.

One of our regulars at the repair shop was a Mr. Kwak. He was about the same age as Mr. Yeo, and his passion for audio equipment meant he had long been a customer of ours. He'd used to be a fireman, but after retirement he said he felt as though he no longer belonged anywhere, and it was around that time that his visits increased in frequency.

Will you take a look at this? Mr. Kwak asked, entering the shop with an old German amp clutched to his chest.

What's the use of looking at that old thing? Mr. Yeo said, but he hunkered down next to Mr. Kwak and proceeded to examine the amp, the two men puffing on their cigarettes companionably.

What's the matter with it? Mr. Yeo asked.

The sound on the left is dead.

How'd you kill it?

I don't know if I killed it, but whatever happened, it's kaput.

It's a solid piece of equipment, though.

Remember that lightning storm we had? I think that's when the problem started.

That's a smart guess.

I'm a smart guy.

All right.

I'll leave it here.

It'll take a while.

The pilot light needs replacing too.

There's no bulb.

I brought one with me.

The bag Mr. Kwak finally fished out of his pocket looked familiar. Mr. Yeo asked him where he'd managed to get his hands on such rare bulbs, and Mr. Kwak said he'd stopped by Omusa on his way. Mr. Yeo and I both goggled at him. Frowning at our evident surprise, Mr. Kwak held the bag of bulbs out to me.

Didn't you know they'd moved? He gave me directions to the new location, a little further down the alley from the original site. The shop itself was identical except that it had a higher ceiling fitted with a tube light, a small sign out front with "Omusa" done in calligraphy, and was, if anything, even more jam-packed than before. The old man was sitting behind his desk, with his back to the shelf of boxes.

Twenty fuse lamps, please, I said, and waited patiently for the familiar slow scrape of the chair as the old man got to his feet.

JUST BEFORE WINTER arrived, it was decided that the first of the five buildings would be torn down.

There was a ribbon-cutting ceremony, attended by reporters and public officials who I'd only ever seen on television or in newspaper photographs. Tucked away to the side of the ceremony itself were the demolition vehicles, draped in banners like babies' bibs, quietly biding their time. I stared at them, at the word "Celebration" emblazoned on the banners. Nothing else was mentioned. I hung around at the back of the crowd for a while, then slipped away and took the lift up to Building B. The next day I stopped at a newsstand on my way to work and saw that all the papers had similar headlines: "Electronics Market Demolished," "Into History," that kind of thing. The one we got delivered to the repair shop was no different. Mr. Yeo spread the paper open on the speaker he used as a table when he ate his meals and read through the article with care, listlessly poking the side dishes with his chopsticks. I asked him why Building A had agreed to the demolition so quickly, and he said that the businesses there were too small-scale. All the traders had been living from hand to mouth, struggling to get by in a building already semi-gutted, with virtually no passing trade; no wonder they didn't bother to quibble when offered a lump sum to move elsewhere.

As for the way the headlines were making it seem as though the entire market had been demolished rather than just one of the five buildings, Mr. Yeo claimed that the intention was to ensure a smooth passage for the final demolition by killing off business in advance. They keep saying Die, die, to those who are already dying, he said, pushing his bowl of jjigae away untouched. Sure enough, in the week following the demolition of Building A, we received several phone calls every day from people saying that they'd read about the market being torn down, and asking if the repair shop had closed or moved.

Unlike the fanfare that surrounded Building B, Building A had been dismantled under cover of night, with tents concealing the machinery.

I saw an article stating that the work would be done using cutting-edge technology, and therefore would be accomplished almost silently. It seemed strange and somewhat suspicious to me that a thirteen-story building could be dismantled so quietly, but when I questioned Mr. Yeo, who worked at the shop until the crack of dawn, he said there'd been no more noise than usual. Each morning I would see that another story had disappeared overnight, the tent had been lowered another level. Once Building A had been fully removed, a park was promptly set up in its place.

In the process, Omusa vanished once more.

It disappeared along with many shops in the area, as the district realigned itself around the park. A faint, scrawny shadow, which may or may not have belonged to the old man, was seen hovering around for several days, still bound by some attachment, but eventually it too was gone. When, feeling sad, I made an excuse to pass by the old Omusa site, I saw abandoned shops with their signs still up, and a now deserted alley with large white Xs daubed on its walls, waiting its turn.

Mr. Yeo and I waited to hear that Omusa had reopened somewhere else, but no such news ever came.

In spring, the landscaping was completed.

The tent was taken down and the park unveiled.

The young grass shoots were green and fresh.

The park was as pretty as a tennis court.

❧

MUJAE AND I stayed late at the market, then went down to the park.

We crept over to one of the benches that had been placed around the park's edge, feeling as though we were doing something forbidden. The bench was long enough to accommodate four people, and in the middle it had a solid horizontal bar that would be taken for an armrest. Why do you think they divided it like this? I asked. They're telling you not to lie down, Mujae said, smiling mysteriously. I smiled back at him. The night was shrouded in fog, but there were tall electric lights only four or five meters apart, so it wasn't too dark.

The lights each had a little cap at the top that made them look like mushrooms, though they also resembled warriors standing guard. Beads of fog clinging to the grass sparkled in the light. I breathed in deeply, and the air felt heavy in my lungs.

Mujae had brought a bag with some food and drink. I picked out a sandwich and a carton of milk. As I ate and drank, my glance fell on the off-limits signs placed here and there on the grass. When I looked left I saw a wide street slicing through the heart of the city, horizontally from east to west, and when I looked right I saw the red outer wall of Building B, newly exposed now that Building A was gone. This wall formed the northern boundary of the park, making it seem as though the park was encroaching on Building B's territory. Having once got lost in Building A, I'd expected a park built in its place to be enormous, but now that I was actually sitting in it, it was smaller than I'd thought. It's not very big, I said, apropos of nothing. Folding his empty milk carton in half, Mujae said that he was surprised, that it was smaller than he'd expected.

All those people, all those shops, were in such a small space.

I wonder where they all went, I said, looking beyond the grass.

Sitting side by side, Mujae and I looked over at the shadow of a newly planted maple tree. It was a night shadow, its edges overlapping with those of the outer dark, and it occurred to me that the old woman with the gray bob must have had her cardboard box lean-to on the patch of ground it covered, or thereabouts. I mentioned her, and Mujae said he'd often seen her. Did you? I said, and then we both fell silent for a time. An insect that looked a bit like a dragonfly only smaller, though it was bigger than a mosquito, described a wobbly ellipse above my knee before landing on the back of my hand. The fog seemed to be weighing heavy on its wings, preventing it from flying properly. I held myself still, watching as it walked up to my wrist then back down to my knuckles, where it hunkered down as though waiting for something with bated breath. Mujae spoke.

Do you know what a slum is, Eungyo?

Something to do with being poor?

I looked it up in a dictionary.

What did it say?

An area in a city where poor people live. Mujae looked at me. They say the area around here is a slum.

Who?

The papers, and people.

Slum?

It's a little odd, isn't it?

It is odd.

Slum.

Slum.

We sat there repeating the word for a while, and then I said, I've heard the word, of course, but I'd never thought of this place as a slum.

I know, right? Mujae sat up a little straighter. My father used to sell stoves here. When I was little, my mother or one of my sisters would bring me with them to visit him, and from a distance, I'd see him sitting in a chair in front of his shop. When we came, he'd disappear off somewhere and come back a little later with steamed blood sausage for us to share. And I'd stand at his side, popping slices of sausage into my mouth and watching the people pass by. I can still see it, as if it were yesterday; him wrapping newspaper around the sausage before he handed it to me, warning that my hands would get greasy, or slipping a few coins into my palm when it was time for me to go home. Thinking back on it now, he was so clumsy, even down to the way he spoke, that it's a wonder he could hold down a business, but I remember that even when we sat there eating sausage he'd stand up whenever someone walked by and ask what they were looking for, if there was anything he could help them with. Sometimes I couldn't hold back the tears; even at that age, I knew enough to feel embarrassed when I saw my father touting, and I hated seeing people walk on by, pretending they couldn't hear him. My father would see my tears and scold me for refusing to explain myself, but I was just upset. He couldn't understand it, and the more he harassed me the harder I'd cry, working myself up into such a state that in the end he just sat there in silence, his head turned away from me. Then the tears would dry up and be replaced by exhaustion. He passed away a long time ago, so you'd think these memories would have faded by now, but they're stubborn as ever, and for me this whole area is inextricably tangled up with those memories and the way they make me feel, and when I hear people call this place a slum, well, it just doesn't seem right to me. Calling a person poor is one thing, that's an objective fact in a way, but "slum" . . . Mujae trailed off.

I wonder if they call this kind of place a slum, because if you called it someone's home or their livelihood that would make things awkward when it comes to tearing it down.

I wonder.

Slum, they say.

Slum.

Slum.

Slum.

Strange, isn't it?

Yeah, it is.

Strange, and a little scary, I said. There was something odd, almost uncanny, about the stark, flat expanse of Building B's newly exposed wall. I stared at it, as if this was the first time I'd realized what a wall was supposed to look like. Even if B disappears, Mujae said, I don't want to move to C. A, B, C, D, E—even if you did move to C, you'd have to pack up again soon enough, down to D and then to E, and after that who knows? Mujae held out the bag. Want some more?

I didn't, so I hesitated, but then reached in and took an orange. Mujae put the bag down and took the orange from me. He peeled it so deftly that the skin splayed out like petals around the navel, then handed it back to me and went on with what he'd been saying.

So I've been looking for somewhere suitable. If we have to move, we might as well make sure there's at least some benefit to it. It was Mr. Gong's idea; he said it was too complicated for him, so he asked me to look into it, and I have, but whenever the place itself seems reasonable the price really isn't, or else it's the other way round. It's not easy.

I handed Mujae two orange segments, which he took and ate.

I'd settle for something like what we have now, but even that's hard to find. When I think about actually having to leave this place and find somewhere else in the area, I feel like what we have now is about the best there is. We're dealing with big lumps of metal at the workshop, so moving further out just isn't an option.

You'll find somewhere.

You think so?

Everybody does.

Where should we go?

It's quiet.

Yeah.

It's pretty, too.

It's pretty, Mujae said, but it feels strange.

Stars and Matryoshkas

WOULD BADMINTON WORK?

Sure, let's do it. I'll bring the rackets.

I didn't mean right now, I said, but Mujae wasn't to be deterred.

I've been having trouble getting to sleep. Do you think exercise might help? It does for me, we'd been saying to each other. Now Mujae told me he was on his way, and hung up. Bewildered, I looked at the clock and saw that it was already past nine o'clock. Did he really mean it? I wondered, but sure enough, half an hour later Mujae cycled up to my house with a water bottle and a pair of badminton rackets.

Let's play.

After hearing that he'd cycled past a dozen bus stops, I thought, never mind badminton, wasn't it enough of a workout just to come all the way here? I kept that thought to myself, and led Mujae to a small park nearby. Full of enthusiasm, he pronounced it the perfect spot.

Have you played badminton before, Eungyo?

I have, I said, but only during P.E. back at primary school, and he told me not to worry, that once you master badminton you never forget it, then handed me a racket and moved away.

Isn't that riding a bike?

I was confused, thinking to myself that Mujae was somehow different today, saying words like "master" and sounding so happy, it was very odd, and then my thoughts were interrupted by Mujae saying, Here goes, and launching the shuttlecock up into the air. I stared blankly as it soared up into the night sky then seemed to hang there, suspended, before dropping down, as though it had needed a moment to make up its mind. I judged that it was about time to hit it, and swung the racket as hard as I could, but it whistled through the empty air and the shuttlecock dropped silently to the ground.

You should keep watching the shuttlecock, Mujae said. You need to watch it till it stops climbing, then after it begins to drop and it feels like you've left it just half a beat late, that's when you swing.

Okay, I said, and served the shuttlecock back to Mujae. The feathers whirled around as it flew through the air. Several times, I sent the shuttlecock over to Mujae only for him to serve it back so high that it whispered straight over my head, no matter how hard I strained to reach. When I complained, Mujae said, It'll drop if you just wait patiently, that's what you need to aim for, almost as if he were teasing me.

We carried on with badminton for a while, taking it in turns to serve with an obligatory "here goes," and then we moved over to the running track. We lined up next to a round sandpit which doubled as a wrestling ring. Let's go, Mujae shouted, and we set off. His long, fluid stride soon carried him out of my sight. The track encircled the park at its outer edge, two hundred and ninety-eight meters in diameter. It had recently been resurfaced, giving it just the right amount of bounce. Running around the track so late at night, lined by still-green maples and ginkgo trees, I wondered what I was doing, out there all by myself. I'd been running for a good while before I heard the soft swish of breath and the thud of shod feet, followed by Mujae calling out my name as he came up behind me. He whisked past before I had time to reply, disappearing around the next corner.

Eungyo!

Eungyo!

After the same thing had happened three times, I decided this wasn't working, turned around and started running the other way. This time, Mujae and I approached each other from opposite ends of the track. Mujae looked baffled when he spotted me. He pulled up and continued to run on the spot.

Why are you coming from that way, Eungyo?

Let's run together.

We are running together.

No we're not, we keep missing each other. This way, we're like satellites with different orbit periods.

Hmm, Mujae frowned, his knees pumping lower each time like a mechanical toy winding down. When he was standing still, he shook his head. You're wrong, Eungyo. If they orbit, they must be planets.

Planets?

Stars are stationary, planets orbit stars, and satellites orbit planets.

But they do both orbit something.

Oh.

Planets orbit, and satellites orbit, right?

That's true, Mujae said. Planets, satellites, hang it, they all orbit. We set off walking, slowly, side by side. Whenever a bicycle needed to pass us either I would duck in behind Mujae or he would move behind me. We were passed by a man and woman who looked like husband and wife, neatly dressed in matching sportswear, then by a woman in a yellow hat who was walking backward, and then by a man in Lycra shorts, who threaded between us with terse concentration as though involved in a race. I spotted the couple who'd passed us earlier heading toward us again.

We're orbiting, too, Eungyo.

We're walking.

We're orbiting as we walk.

Seems like just walking to me.

But even if we are just walking, when it comes down to it, the fact that the earth is round means we're also orbiting.

That makes the scale too big, Mujae.

And could be either planets or satellites, like you said.

What could?

We could.

We walked in silence for a while. Even though it was getting late, a fair number of people were out exercising. Some were doing freehand exercises like squats or push-ups, some were using the equipment provided or a skipping rope they'd brought with them, or running along the track in the light of the streetlamps. I'd thought we'd left our earlier conversation pretty much wrapped up, so Mujae's next remark struck me as somewhat out of the blue.

What would you rather be, Eungyo, a planet or a satellite?

I don't want to be something that orbits.

How about a comet, then?

Don't comets have orbits too? Halley's comet does.

Halley's comet, Mujae repeated quietly, seeming to mull it over for a while. He perked up. How about a meteor? Wouldn't it be good to be a meteor?

But meteors burn up and disappear. It seems so futile.

That's because it is so futile.

We made a few more circuits of the track, then stopped at the park's eastern entrance where Mujae had tied up his bike. Do you think you'll be able to fall asleep now? I asked, and he said he thought he might. We said good-bye and Mujae pedaled forward a couple of meters before putting his left foot down and looking back over his shoulder. Actually, Eungyo, I was wrong earlier.

About what?

Stars aren't stationary. They move. At that, Mujae set off again, wobbling away into the distance.

The next day, at the electronics market, I asked Mujae if he'd slept well.

His only answer was a vague smile.

⌐

EACH WEEK A fair was held in the park that had replaced Building A.

The preparations began on Friday mornings, with the arrival of vans loaded with iron beams, lighting equipment, and so on. By noon, the stage was set up on the grass. Wooden boards, skillfully crafted so as not to damage the grass, formed a floor for the audience to sit on. A little past noon, the speakers would be tested a couple of times before the music began to play. And then there was the fair's host shouting into the microphone against the background of the audience's growing din, so loud it made your head ring. As Building B faced directly onto the park, even closing the repair shop windows couldn't shut out the noise, so we simply had to grit our teeth and bear it, counting down the hours until the event was finally over. Once the music started up Mr. Yeo lost his ability to concentrate, eventually giving up and heading down to the pool hall to wait it out, swearing under his breath. It was too stiflingly hot to keep the windows closed for long, but with them open it was too loud for me to do anything but sit there in a daze, gazing dumbly at Mujae's seed leaves dancing about on top of the cabinet.

Ostensibly as part of the fair, tents were set up outside Building B's northern wall, blocking the main access road to the market. On the other side of the tents the music continued to be pumped out, as though reassuring everyone that there was nothing to worry about. The louder it grew on the other side of the tents, the darker and quieter it grew in Building B, as if the very existence of the latter was slowly being effaced. Banners were hung on the building's southern wall and notices put up inside next to the lifts, all for some reason looking rather slapdash, stating that Building B had been in business for forty years and would continue to be so for at least another twenty.

The negotiations over Building B seemed to be progressing at a snail's pace. Some said that this was because, unlike Building A, Building B had no majority owner, with each of its numerous tenants having an equal stake. Word went around that they were reluctant to sell at the prices being offered by public enterprises, which had been hit hard by the downturn in the real estate business, and therefore Building B would be divided into various sections, with public enterprises occupying just a few units at the back and private enterprises entrusted with the rest. Hearing how each unit could be expected to fetch two or three hundred million won, I felt like I was listening to a fairytale in a foreign language.

What do they mean by private enterprises? I asked Mr. Yeo.

Private means money.

Money?

Money is a powerful thing. Mr. Yeo said that the government had made a show of digging up the first shovelful themselves, then quietly handed over the shovel; that that was how they'd always been, and that nothing ever changes. Then he swore a couple of times. Lately, he said, the shadows have been starting to dominate.

Some days when he came to work it was his shadow that went ahead of him.

DO YOU WANT some chicken?

Mujae came by the repair shop on Saturday with some fried chicken. Mr. Yeo had told me to lock up, and gone down to the pool hall. We arranged the food on top of an upturned speaker. A song was being pumped out from the direction of the park, an innocent refrain about tomatoes being good for your health. We had to raise our voices if we wanted to be heard properly, which was embarrassing, so we soon gave up and applied ourselves to the chicken. It was hot and crispy and had soaked up just the right amount of soy sauce. Each time I picked up a piece Mujae chimed in with "That's a wing," or "That's a breast," or "That's a breast, too."

Help yourself, Eungyo, he said.

I am.

Who wants the neck?

I don't eat necks.

Shall I?

The neck was about the size of Mujae's index finger, which he used to pinch it with his thumb. He sucked on it first, then put it in his mouth and crunched it with his teeth, spitting out tiny discs of bone one by one into his hand.

What does it taste like?

It tastes like chicken.

Not like neck?

What does neck taste like, Eungyo? Mujae asked with his mouth full.

Never mind. I'm sorry.

No, I'm curious.

It tastes like lead.

Lead?

Because the neck is the part of the body where all our exhaustion gathers, like a lead weight dragging it down. So that's why I thought it must taste like lead.

I see.

I'm sorry, you're eating.

It's not a problem, Mujae said, but he was frowning as he munched on his chicken and seemed to have a lot on his mind, so I genuinely regretted what I'd said. Now that I think about it, Mujae said, chickens must have the highest stress levels of all the living things that humans consume. And there are so many of them.

Mujae carefully extracted a thin bone from his mouth and examined it closely before placing it on a napkin. The song about tomatoes being healthy vegetables had come to an end, so we were able to speak in our normal voices.

Last night, Mujae said, I stumbled on a shadow.

What?

I stumbled, Mujae said. And I fell.

I WENT HOME late last night. I didn't realize how late it was until I got home and looked at the clock, wondering why my feet were aching so badly, even more than they usually do. I slumped down by the front door for a while, gathering the energy to go and wash myself, then hauled myself up. I took a couple of steps toward the bathroom, stumbled and fell. I'd tripped over something, only there was nothing to trip over. But then I looked and saw the edge of my shadow, risen about half a handspan up off the floor. There was still a faint swatch on the floor—a shadow of a shadow—but the blackness that had peeled up from it was slightly more vivid. So that's how a shadow looks when it rises, I thought to myself.

I touched it.

I thought it'd be thin and flimsy like paper, but it wasn't. I can't describe exactly what it did feel like, Eungyo, not to you now and not to myself even at the time. No matter how many times I touched it, it just felt vague. Maybe a newly risen shadow is a very vague thing. I thought that my shadow had risen a little higher while I'd been examining it, but I was tired, so I just got on with the various things I needed to do and left it to its own devices. I moved here and there about the house, but my shadow didn't accompany my body. Instead, it remained fixed in place, so it felt as though my center had naturally shifted to the risen shadow, meaning I couldn't help but be conscious of it, like an ankle shackled by a chain, or a dog tied to a leash, or a compass that can't not know where north is. And all the while my shadow was rising slightly higher. When I took a last look before going to bed it was raised up from the floor at an acute angle. I could clearly make out a head and shoulders, and the beginnings of a left arm.

And did you sleep? I asked.

I did, Mujae said. I finally felt sleep come over me last night, so I thought it'd be a waste not to give in.

So that was that? Mujae shook his head.

Not quite, he said. I woke up in the middle of the night, I was thirsty and my chest felt tight; I'd been dreaming, though I couldn't remember what about; pain radiated from the crown of my head, as if I'd been napping in a stifling room; I lay there for a while, having completely forgotten about the shadow; the floor was cold and it felt as if some heavy thing was tugging at my back, so I rolled onto my side, but as I did so something attached itself to me, clinging so tightly I could barely even twitch my limbs; it was incredibly strong, too strong for me to shuck it off by rolling over or pin it beneath me by lying flat; I struggled, feeling it push back more violently, and then I heard it whispering something and when I strained to listen I could make out the words *anyway, anyway*; the hairs stood up on the back of my neck and I struggled with all my might, thinking I'd be done for if I let my guard down for even a moment; I struggled not to lie down under its violent force, and took the first chance I got to roll over onto my back. Suddenly it was all over, there was no force pushing or pulling at me anymore and no sign of what had caused it; I couldn't tell if I'd had a nightmare or if I'd been wrestling with my shadow.

Anyway, I couldn't get back to sleep after that, Mujae said.

❧

THAT NIGHT, I had trouble falling asleep too.

The sun was almost up when I finally managed it, sleeping until past noon. It was a fine day, so I went for a cycle to try and shake my feelings of frustration and claustrophobia. I went slowly at first, pedaling leisurely down the same road I often took, then, deciding that it would be a shame to waste the weather, I set out for Mujae's house. I whizzed past a dozen bus stops, noticing several junctions and busy streets that would be tricky to navigate on a bike. A strange nostalgia swept over me as I realized that Mujae must pass these same places every night. I could see him in my mind's eye, cycling away that night we went to the park. I pedaled diligently. I pulled up in front of a pharmacy, leaned the bike against the wall and called Mujae's home; after a brief, desultory exchange, I mentioned that I happened to be in the area, and a couple of minutes later there was Mujae in the street, walking toward me in a loose T-shirt and shorts.

I couldn't help but stare at the squat noon shadow that dogged his steps, lengthening and contracting in a flexible rhythm. Up close, he looked disheveled and exhausted. I stared at him, hesitating whether to ask him how he'd slept, and he stared back at me.

Have you had lunch? Mujae asked after a while.

I told him I hadn't.

Let's make some cold noodles, Mujae said, and I followed him off the main road into a small, quiet market.

There were so many things I wanted to say, but I didn't know how to put them into words, so I was flustered, constantly fidgeting with the handlebars of my bike, whereas Mujae calmly picked out a radish then asked if we should get chives or spring onions.

Well, I said, still flustered, does it matter? They're both green, aren't they? And they're both alliums.

Mujae frowned, saying that they were different shapes and that the taste of each was quite distinct, mulled it over a little more, then picked up a bunch of chives.

It's this way, he said.

He led us through the market to a narrow building sandwiched between two others. On the ground floor was a shabby restaurant specializing in wheat noodle soup. A shallow pond had been carved out by the entrance; its three goldfish were motionless at the bottom, save for the occasional twitch of a fin. We found some railings to tie up my bicycle, then climbed the narrow staircase to the fourth floor, opened a small door and walked out onto the rooftop. An enclosed space had been constructed using orange bricks, where a clothesline had been strung up and a small washing machine was humming quietly. I went over to the railing and looked down onto the market we'd just passed through. People were coming and going beneath the faded flags of various countries. The midday sun seemed to bore into my eyes, making it hard to think straight. This is a good place for drying laundry, I thought, then shook my head as though it had water in it when Mujae came out with the exact same words. I took off my shoes and lined them up on the purple tiles by the door, then stepped up onto the raised wooden floor. Mujae's home was mainly empty space, with no real furniture to speak of. There was a radio and a telephone, a chest of drawers stacked with folded blankets, a plate bearing the remains of a mosquito coil, and, by the door, a flowerpot planted with electronic chips and copper wires. I asked him why he hadn't planted flowers instead, and he said they weren't planted, it was just that he sometimes came home to find that such things had ended up in his pockets, so he stuck them in the flowerpot to stop himself from treading on them. This was exactly what happened whenever I left similar things lying around. I examined the flowerpot carefully, wondering if I ought to get one for myself. Mujae rummaged in the cupboard for something while I looked around the space. There was a large, west-facing window, which made the room light and airy, its yellow curtain somewhat frayed at the bottom. Plates and bowls were stacked upside down in the small sink, and a strange gleam next to this caught my eye.

∾

IS THAT ONE of those self-righting dolls? I asked, but Mujae said no, it's a matryoshka. It was the size of a rice jar, and had a girl with a red kerchief painted onto it. Mujae said that one of his sisters had been given it as a gift, but when she got married her husband said it freaked him out, so she'd given it to Mujae for safekeeping. I'd never seen a matryoshka before, and gaped in wonder as Mujae put his hand on its round head.

Shall we open it?

Can we?

Why not?

Ensconced in the shadow of the first matry-oshka was a second, slightly smaller copy. Mujae twisted the second matryoshka's head off with a click, and there inside was another shadow, cra-dling a third matryoshka. As Mujae worked his way through the matryoshkas I took their upper halves from him one at a time and arranged them on the floor around us. The girls' round faces shone in the sun, some wreathed in smiles and some in tears, some wearing expressions of blank incomprehension and some whose mouths formed a small o of surprise. The kinds of clothes they wore, the patterns on their headscarves, their hair and eye color were each slightly different from that of the others. I asked Mujae how many there were altogether, and he handed me the upper half of the twelfth matryoshka while peering down at the newly revealed thirteenth.

About twenty-nine, I think.

That's a lot.

Should we go on opening them?

We agreed that we might as well, now we'd started. Click, click, click, click, click. When twenty-eight upper halves dotted the floor, only the final matryoshka remained. It had the rich brown gloss of an acorn, but was smaller than a pea. The barest suggestion of a mouth and eyebrows had been painted onto its face, which could equally have been that of a newborn baby or of an ancient woman. Mujae held it out to me. It dropped onto my palm light as a rice puff, indescribably light, just a thin shell enclosing an empty space. I tilted my palm like a pinball table and watched the matryoshka roll along the creases, but I was a little too reckless with the angle—the matryoshka skimmed off the edge of my hand, and I stepped forward to catch it but ended up stepping on it instead.

I froze, a brief sound escaping before I clamped my lips together, and Mujae bent to gather the shattered pieces, pressing his fingertip down on the tiniest ones like picking up candy crumbs. The fragments could no longer be called a matryoshka, or even a simple nut. The damage was irreparable.

It's broken.

Mujae, I'm sorry.

It's all right.

I'm sorry.

He shook the bits into a bin like so many crumbs and set to work closing up the matryoshkas, each click a little louder, a little more emphatic, than when he'd opened them.

Click.

Click.

Click.

Click.

Eventually there was only one matryoshka, concealing one less layer than it had before. I'm sorry, I said again, and Mujae said, It's all right, nothing to worry about, then turned on the tap to wash the radish.

〜

THE THING ABOUT matryoshkas, Mujae announced while he grated the radish, is that they're hollow to begin with. There's nothing inside of any substance. There's just one matryoshka inside another, that repetition is itself what defines a matryoshka, not any actual object part, so in fact it's more precise to say that a matryoshka contains an eternal recurrence than a number of smaller matryoshkas. So it's not as though anything has ceased to exist because it broke; all we've done is confirmed that it never existed in the first place.

That sounds so futile, Mujae.

Futility is precisely why I've always thought that a matryoshka resembles human life.

The radish had been reduced to the size of a fist, and Mujae used it to point at the matryoshka.

I've always thought that's what life boils down to. Little by little, seeing all the shadows rising around me, I consumed these thoughts, or should I say I became consumed by them. How about this story, for instance. When I was in middle school I lived with my mother and sisters, in a part of town where not many other people lived and even fewer visited, except if they'd taken a wrong turn in their car, because it was far from any main road and didn't lead on to anywhere else. Behind our house lived an old lady who went around collecting discarded cardboard boxes to sell, but one day she had a run-in with an old man who'd come from another area to scavenge boxes, and they got into a fight. I went outside to see what all the fuss was about, and saw the two of them facing off in the middle of the street, arguing loudly over a heap of boxes and rags. They used swear words

I'd never even heard before and cursed each other viciously, tearing rags from each other's handcart and hurling them away into the street. The old man slunk off after a while, leaving the woman to her spoils. I watched her as she shuffled back into her house, thumping her chest, her face twisted with resentment. I saw her shadow hanging over her, its hugely swollen head outlined against the breeze-block wall, its concrete festooned with trumpet creepers. She left her handcart in the middle of the street. It was still there hours later, when night fell, which did make me wonder, but I left it at that, and only later found out that the old woman had died that same day. Some locals found her sprawled out in her yard. The grown-ups told us that her heart had seized up from a chronic disease, but I overheard them whispering among themselves about how the old woman's shadow had hounded her to death. Even after her children came and held a funeral for her, her handcart re-mained where she'd left it. There wasn't much in it, just a few boxes, lumps of Styrofoam and torn sheets of plastic, and as I looked at it I thought,

A person can die for the sake such things, a person can die and this is all they leave behind, feeling like something had fastened its teeth into me and bitten a chunk out of my side. That's the story, anyway.

Mujae was gazing steadily into the simmering broth, clutching a handful of dry buckwheat noodles.

Eungyo, I don't really think there's another world after death, and I thought it was inevitable for a person to feel more or less hollow, no matter their individual circumstances. The essence of human life, if there is such a thing, is futility, that's the way it's always been and the way it always will be, and so there's no call to make a fuss about it. That's what I thought, anyway. But lately, my thoughts have been somewhat different.

Different in what way? I asked.

For instance, is it really so natural and inevitable for an old woman to eke out a living by scavenging cardboard boxes? Is that part of the essence of human life? Is dying like that down to the individual, nothing to do with anyone else? And if it's not natural and inevitable, just sufficiently common to be accepted as such, isn't that futility even worse than if it was simply the essence of life?

✦

EUNGYO, IT'LL BE too sharp if you put in so much radish and spring onion.

I like it sharp.

It'll be too sharp.

Mujae scooped out a spoonful of the mixture from my bowl and poured in some soybean broth. Ice cubes clamored to the surface, and I added some of the noodles. Mujae and I ate in silence. The ice chilled the noodles so severely that my teeth ached whenever I had to chew. Sunlight streamed in through the open door, slanting onto a corner of the table. Every so often, presumably due to clouds shifting in front of the sun, that bright patch would abruptly darken. I sat there watching it for a while, and when I looked up again I saw Mujae's shadow, risen. It was there by his side, smaller than he was and similar in shape, but the face was dark and dry, couldn't really be called a face. Mujae was lost in thought, leaving the shadow unchallenged. Mujae, I said, but his expression remained blank as he continued to move the cold noodles into his mouth.

Mujae.

Mujae.

With a lump in my throat, I called his name in a voice so faint that I wondered whether I was actually producing any sound. The shadow slid one arm onto the table. Its black hand, strangely elongated but with defined fingers, seemed pointed toward me. I thought it might reach out to me, but it remained where it was, unmoving.

I held myself equally still. Now that his shadow had risen, it seemed as though Mujae was no longer present. He looked faint, and there was something vague about his movements, even though they were entirely ordinary, transferring noodles to his mouth, chewing them slowly and swallowing them down. Sometimes the passing clouds must have been quite large, as it would take some time for our surroundings to brighten again. As the room shifted between light and dark the shadow gradually sank back down. It went back to being the kind of shadow that is subordinate to the body, its movements only echoes. Cicadas chirred in chorus, a sound like metal grating on stone. Mujae was busy removing a lump of mustard that was clinging to his noodles. I used my chopsticks to tweezer a piece of pickled cucumber, but my hand was trembling and I ended up dropping it into my soup. I stared at it, chopsticks hovering in midair.

Eungyo, Mujae said, your soup will get salty if you leave that there.

It's all right.

Do you want a fresh batch?

No.

Are you full?

No.

What's wrong?

Mujae.

Eungyo?

I want a different kind of soup, not cold like this, something hot and clear and refreshing that heats you up from the inside, and lots of it. I sniffed, wiped my nose and finished my noodles.

A soft alarm sounded, indicating that the washer had finished its spin cycle.

Island

IN THAT CASE, LET'S GO and have some hot and clear
and refreshing soup, Mujae said. I thought he was
suggesting we go out right then, maybe to one of
the clam noodle restaurants nearby, but it was the
following weekend when he called me at home.

I'm leaving now, so meet me in eight minutes.

That was all he said before he hung up, which
happened so fast I didn't even get the chance to
ask where were supposed to meet. Hastily blast-
ing my hair with the hand dryer, I wondered how
he'd managed to come up with not five or ten but
precisely eight minutes, which I was still puzzling
over when those eight minutes were up. I opened

the window and looked out, but I couldn't see Mujae anywhere. Not knowing how far we might be going, I slipped on a pair of old flip-flops and went outside. Mujae was standing at the entrance to the alley, leaning against a car whose ability to drive without falling apart looked dubious at best. Mujae beckoned to me and I ran over. Let's go get some soup, Mujae said, opening the passenger door for me. I was laughing so much I had to clutch my sides.

Mujae, I spluttered, did you find this thing in a dump?

Mujae grinned from ear to ear.

We set off in search of some soup, something hot and clear and refreshing. Bouncing up and down in the sagging seat, I fiddled with the mirror and rummaged through the door compartment. There, I found a notebook with an insurance card slipped between its pages, a single cotton work glove, and two cassette tapes of childrens' songs. Mujae said that everything except the insurance card belonged to the car's previous owner, who'd bought himself a new used car just last week, which sounded weird, a new used car, but in any case, that's how he'd become a car owner, for only thirty thousand won, the price of a decent toaster. That's so cheap! I exclaimed, and Mujae said, That's because it's such a wreck! The engine made such a terrific din, it sounded as though the car was hurling a stream of curses at the other vehicles. I pushed the button to lower my window, only to discover that the mechanism only worked one way; I tried pulling it back up with my hands, but had to give up and leave it as it was. It was fun. Even the wind whipping my hair over my face was fun. When Mujae braked for a red light the car juddered like it was having a seizure.

It's shaking!

It is!

We both roared with laughter.

It was odd to be so excited by riding in a beat-up car, but I was happy, which made me laugh out loud, happy to be happy.

What kind of soup are we having? I asked.

Clam soup, of course, if you want something clear and refreshing.

Manila clams?

Manila clams, yes, and other clams too.

Other clams?

There are plenty of clams besides manila clams, Eungyo. There's scallops, king clams, hen clams, venus clams, razor clams, butter clams, ark clams, hard clams, surf clams, and short-necked clams, Mujae said, skillfully maneuvering the car through the traffic as he rattled off this list of names, some of which I'd heard before and some of which were completely new. The afternoon sun sparkled on the car bonnet, on those bits of paint that weren't chipped off.

Are we going to eat all those clams, Mujae?

That's right.

Wow.

Are you happy?

Yes.

I'm happy that you're happy.

I'm happy that I'm happy, too.

Chatting in this way, we crossed the provincial boundary.

AT THE DOCK we were given a map, which showed how the island resembled a sock, carefully re-moved so as to retain its shape. The map also clarified that the island itself had two docks in total, one at the southern end and one at the east, ports both large and small, and had once boasted a number of salt fields, though only one now remained. I repeated those words to myself, salt fields, while Mujae announced that the boat had arrived and turned on the car's engine. We crawled onto the deck, rumbling and clattering. The boat ride took about twenty minutes, so we decided to go out on deck rather than stay sitting in the car. We stood by ourselves, a little way off from the people feeding seagulls, and watched the dock recede into the distance as the boat moved further out. Behind the concrete tetrapods that formed a breakwater, the cars that hadn't been able to fit onto the boat were lined up. From somewhere in the bowels of the boat came a continuous thump, thump, thumping sound, as though the keel was knocking into something, though the boat kept moving slowly but steadily forward, churning a reddish-brown wake. Mujae and I held on to the railing, less giddy than when we'd first started out.

This boat is as much of a wreck as your car, Mujae.

I moved toward the bow to get a different view, somewhat disoriented at first by the sight of a very similar dock not receding but approaching. The breakwater on the island was just a narrow strip, sloping up to a road that forked in two. We went back to the car and waited our turn; we'd been one of the first to drive onto the boat, so we were among the last to disembark. At the fork, Mujae took the right-hand road without hesitation. We drove along with the sea to our right and a rocky mountain path to our left. The rice paddies to our left looked to be lower than sea level.

They say the rice here tastes especially good because it grows in the breeze from the sea, Mujae said.

I stuck my head out of the window and peered at the waves, the wind forcing me to squint.

Eungyo, it's dangerous to stick your head out like that.

I can see better this way.

There'll be a much better view from the lookout point.

Are we going there?

Why not? Mujae said, then added, After we have some soup. We drove through a wide field flanked by paddies and arrived at a small port. A cobbled breakwater stretched down to the mud flats, with a cluster of single-level shacks specializing in raw fish. We went into the first one and ordered clam soup. Neither Mujae nor I was a fan of raw fish, but the owner insisted on serving us some raw shrimp, saying they'd been caught that same morning. As we savored the creamy sweetness of the shrimps' transparent flesh, a large pot was delivered to our table, chock-full of fist-sized clams. Once the clams had cooked fully in the boiling soup, Mujae fished them out and put them on my plate, naming each one in turn.

This one's a scallop, this is a king clam, this is a butter clam, no, wait, a hard clam . . . or a butter clam, perhaps? The clams alone were enough to fill me up, and toward the end of the meal I grew drowsy, almost nodding off with my spoon still in my hand. The window behind Mujae was open onto the sea, the tide so far out that all that could be seen were the gleaming mud flats. Several fishing boats were stranded near the shore, sticking out of the mud all askew. Does the tide come in as far as those boats? I asked Mujae, and the owner stuck his head out of the kitchen and answered, It comes right up to the window. If the sea comes right up to the window, I pondered drowsily, what happens when there's a typhoon? What will happen to all the people? When the sun began to redden we left the breakwater and walked back to the car.

Did you like the soup? Mujae asked. Was it hot and refreshing enough for you?

Yes, I liked it, and yes, it was hot and clear and refreshing. Thank you for bringing me here, Mujae, I said, and Mujae smiled.

I'VE BEEN HERE before, you know, Mujae said as he drove us toward the island's western corner.

When? I asked.

A couple of times when I was in college.

You went to college?

I did, but I quit pretty quickly. I didn't think what I was learning there was worth getting into debt for.

Mujae turned into a temple compound and parked the car. The path leading up the mountain had a steep gradient, and was so narrow that two cars would have only just squeezed past each other. It was flanked by basic shacks selling mung bean pancakes and unfiltered rice wine. A couple of places had touts outside, turning smelt on a brazier while calling out to passersby to come and enjoy a meal. The narrow path was thronged with temple-goers, most of whom seemed to have come in big groups. The air was thick with the smell of frying eggs. Mujae and I walked up to the temple's entrance, a single-pillar gate of ancient, weathered wood, where a woman wearing blackened gloves was handing something out to everyone who went by. Just to taste, she said as she dropped one in my hand, and it turned out to be a chestnut, small as an acorn and with the same shiny shell. It had been scored at the top and roasted over charcoal.

How is it? Mujae asked.

So good, I mumbled with my mouth full. Mujae darted back to the gate and returned with a bag of chestnuts.

Crack, crack, I shelled the chestnuts and popped the yellow kernels into my mouth as I puffed my way up the slope. It was so steep that I wondered how we'd get back down without tumbling head over heels. I was so busy chomping on chestnuts than I kept having to stop and catch my breath, so Mujae soon overtook me. I looked up when he called my name and saw him there at the top of the slope, looking oddly lonely.

Are they that good, Eungyo?

They really are.

What's so great about them?

I hurried up the last of the slope while Mujae waited for me.

A flight of stone steps led up from the temple grounds, zigzagging up the mountainside. After one hundred and eighty steps I stopped counting and just concentrated on moving my legs. My calves were soon aching so badly that it was an effort even to lift my feet up, but just when I was thinking I would have to stop I stumbled onto flat ground. There was an observation deck with long wooden benches and, higher up, a round-faced Buddha had been carved into a steep rock face. A flat rock jutted out above the Buddha's head like a mushroom cap. Mujae and I climbed right up to the statue, but we were worried about disturbing those who had spread out mats to pray, so we came back down to the observation deck.

A cat! someone cried out, and we followed their pointing finger to find a pregnant black cat gracefully navigating the steep slope, padding through a carpet of fallen leaves.

The observation deck jutted out from a high bluff, overhanging the sea. The sun was just beginning to set. Mujae and I sat side by side with our backs to the Buddha statue, gazing out at the lilac-tinged water. The sky was a subtle blend of blues, yellows and reds, merging hazily with the sea at the horizon. I could see the parking lot, much further away than I'd thought, and beyond that the mud flats and the one remaining salt field. The tide hadn't yet come in, so the mud flats still stretched on into the distance. The abandoned salt field was red, though I couldn't guess the reason. Each island, a sparse, dream-like smattering on the vast sea, bore a tall electricity pylon. Like objects seen in a rear-view mirror, the islands and their towers seemed nearer than they were in reality, fading away little by little and leaving me utterly rapt, wondering where the electric current went when it passed beyond the sea.

The sky looks amazing, Mujae sighed.

It really does.

Whenever I see this kind of scene, I always end up thinking that humans are truly strange creatures.

Strange?

They're needlessly loud and always in a rush, and violent too, in many ways.

That sounds more like the description of a city to me.

A city? Mujae thought for a moment, then laughed. In any case, a scene like this comforts me because it feels set apart from anything human.

Some soft thing brushed against my calf. I looked down and saw the same black cat rubbing herself against me. Her swollen belly was taut as a drumskin. Mujae carefully picked her up and put her on his lap. Her fur was matted with bark and grass seeds which Mujae began to remove, breaking off to stroke her when she twitched and fidgeted. After a while she narrowed her eyes, settled down and began to purr. It was strange seeing Mujae with a cat in his lap, hunched on a cliff near the top of a mountain. There were still some people climbing up to the Buddha, though the steady stream had slowed to a trickle. They even stick pylons in places like that, Mujae murmured, staring out over the sea.

THE SUN SANK lower in the sky as we made our way back down to the gate. I discovered the solution to my earlier conundrum—it was possible to walk down the slope without toppling over, but only by leaning as far back as we could go. By the time we reached the car dusk had fallen all around us. Half the shacks selling smelt and raw rice wine were closing up for the day, and the rest already had their doors shut and lights out. Mujae switched on the headlamps and swung the car out of the parking lot then down to the main road. I had the nagging feeling that I'd left something behind; I craned my neck to look in the rearview mirror, but all I could see were twin lines of telephone poles receding into the gathering dark. Mujae had grown considerably less talkative, and our silence was flooded by the noise from the car's engine as it carried us forward over the island. The streetlights were set much further apart than in the city, and disappeared altogether after a certain point. We drove with a great blackness to our left which we assumed to be the sea. Occasionally, the car's interior would be dimly illuminated by lights from cuttlefish boats far out to sea, but these were only brief interruptions, as the road would soon dip down below hills or duck away inland.

Do you think we've missed the last boat, Mujae?

We haven't.

We shouldn't have, right?

There are still two more, the last one and the second to last.

Even after hearing that we still had plenty of time, I felt uneasy.

What are you so worried about, Eungyo?

It's too dark.

Of course it's dark, it's nighttime.

But it's so dark it doesn't seem possible that we'll make it to somewhere bright.

That's nonsense, Eungyo, what's got into you?

I know it's nonsense, Mujae, but I can't help thinking it. The words were barely out of my mouth when the car's headlights bounced off a sign announcing the dock.

There now, what did I say?

Mujae turned in to the dock, but it was still ominously dark. The glimpses afforded by our headlights revealed a quite different scene from what I remembered. To our right was the dark hump of a mountain which we definitely hadn't seen when we'd disembarked. There were no lights on to signal to incoming boats, and it was equally dark across the water, where the mainland dock should have been waiting. There were no other cars waiting for a boat. We stayed there alone in the quiet dark, trying to understand what had happened. I felt as though someone had cast a spell on us, until I recalled that the dock we'd arrived at was relatively new, built to replace an old one further to the south. The dock the map had said was derelict.

This must be the old dock, Mujae.

Ah, he said, then we must have taken the wrong turning at the fork.

What do we do?

It's all right, Eungyo, the new dock isn't far away. Mujae turned the car around and drove out of the dock, but we hadn't gotten far before the engine's habitual rumbling turned into a death rattle, followed by an eerie silence.

⌒

THE ONLY LANDMARK was a solitary streetlamp in the otherwise empty darkness.

The emergency light was blinking and there was a smell like burnt dust. Mujae got out first, and after a few beats I followed him. Thankfully, the car had rolled to a gradual stop rather than a violent crash. Loose wisps of smoke snaked up from under the bonnet, dispersing swiftly in the wind. A black, viscous spillage was spreading silently from beneath the car. While Mujae opened the hood and examined the engine, I walked around to the rear and looked back in the direction from which we'd come. Both behind us and in front of us was engulfed in the same utter black. I looked from one direction to the other, then tipped my head back to gaze up at the sky. Dark as it was, I couldn't see many stars, just the hazy, red-tinged sliver of a waning moon. The wind smelled of salt and fish.

I'm sorry, Mujae said. I couldn't see him, so I walked back round to the front of the car. He was crouched with his chin in his hand, elbow resting on his knees. He seemed to be examining the bumper, but when I went up to him he said again, I'm sorry, his voice still faint and despondent. I'm sorry things turned out this way. I wanted to ask him what he had to be sorry for, but I thought that would just make him apologize again, so instead I said, It's okay, it's okay, then turned away to face into the dark, the vast field stretching out around us.

There were no tall structures that I could make out, just some low-slung shapes that might have been fences or walls. I sensed an even wider expanse beyond the field, and I realized what it meant to be an island.

As I turned around I nearly stepped on Mujae's shadow. The car bonnet was still propped open, and Mujae was on his feet now, peering inside. He was silent, and the dense weave of his shadow stretched from his heels to the edge of the road, giving off a feeling different from that of other things that were there. At the radius of the streetlamp's puddled light the darkness of the field sucked up the shadow, so I couldn't tell where the shadow ended and the darkness began. It seemed as though the island itself were Mujae's shadow.

Mujae! I called his name, but he made no reply.

The light haloing his bowed head only served to emphasize the night that lay beyond it. I looked up at the streetlamp, feeling lost and afraid. The metal hemisphere capping the bulb looked like an upturned bowl, or perhaps a mouth. The mouth of the darkness. It had to have one somewhere. And whenever it chose to close that mouth, Mujae and the light would go poof and vanish. Setting my back to the darkness, that seemed to tug at the nape of my neck, I walked toward Mujae. I took his hand, which felt cold and hard, more like a bone than living flesh. Even if it is a bone, it's Mujae's bone, I thought, squeezing as though our lives depended on it.

Mujae.

Mujae.

Shall we walk? I said, and finally he turned to look at me.

Where to?

To the dock.

It's so dark, you don't know who we might run into. Could be anyone.

Anyone would do, I said, that's why we're going. I'd be happy to run in to anyone right now. And if we do, won't they be just as startled, given that we could be anyone too?

We'll have missed the last boat.

Even so, there must be people who live around there. Let's go, I said, pulling him by the hand, and he began to move forward without much resistance. His hand felt both heavy and insubstantial in mine, and I felt strangely alone.

When we'd moved a little way beyond the streetlamp's aureole, Mujae said, Wait, and returned to the car. He got a hazard triangle out of the boot and set it up facing the direction from which we'd come, the stretch of road that led from the derelict dock. He came back and slipped his hand into mine. We promised the car that we'd return with help as soon as we found some, then turned away, still holding hands. The sound of the blinking emergency light gradually faded away. As we moved beyond the light's reach, the density of the air and the feel of the wind seemed to alter. From time to time we looked back over our shoulders at the car huddled beneath the streetlamp. Next to it, a tall, slender shadow was swaying. It was a fair distance away by now, and the darkness had obliterated the ground, making it impossible to tell whether it was Mujae's or mine. It wavered on the spot as though hesitating over some action, then slowly began to move in our direction. It passed into the darkness from the edge of the light and vanished from our eyes.

It's following us, I thought, and this thought, that a shadow was following us, didn't strike the least fear in me. At the top of a low rise we saw streetlamps twinkling in the distance. There were three of them, leading toward a bend in the road. Walking through the darkness that lay outside the light I felt as though the path we passed along was floating in midair. Are we ghosts? we wondered.

Who could tell, this late at night. We might be ghosts seeking others of our kind, walking under a pale moon.

We walked slowly on, alternately engulfed in darkness and exposed by light.

Eungyo, Mujae said. Shall we sing?

Interview with
Hwang Jungeun

This story was in part inspired by the Yong-san apartment building disaster in 2009; for readers who might not be familiar, can you explain what happened in Yongsan? What kind of social and economic factors played a role in the tragedy?

Following the end of Imperial Japan's colonial occupation, the Korean War scorched the entire country. After the war, both the Korean government and its people deemed economic growth a crucial mission, as "making a living" had become essential. This trend has persisted for over seventy years since the ceasefire declaration. The emphasis on economic value (money) has consistently over-shadowed our rights to labor safety, life, and stable housing, among others. Hence occasional disasters in recent history.

The Yongsan disaster was one such case. Yongsan was Seoul's redevelopment district at the time; residents of the area were evicted, and their homes and businesses were to be demolished. The day before the incident, people driven out by the redevelopment project occupied one of the buildings in protest, demanding adequate compensation for their displacement and demonstrating for their right to life and housing. Authority figures, including police officers, enlisted the help of dubious civilians known as "gangsters for hire" to halt the protests with violent measures and excessive force, instead of following the existing protocols.

In the end, a fire broke out during the raid; six people died—five civilians and a police officer—and twenty-three more were injured.

I sat in on and wrote about a case where the survivors of this incident were convicted. The following is an excerpt of "A Mouth-Eating Mouth," first published in the 2009 winter issue of *Munhakdongne Quarterly*:

On Monday morning, January 19th, the area in the vicinity of the Namildang building was flagged by the police, with civilians not permitted to enter the alleyway. But the private enforcement agents crossed the police line and entered the Namildang building. They spent over eight hours inside, breaking down the barriers erected by the protesters to halt their advance and starting a fire on a staircase to funnel smoke up to the rooftop. A fire engine arrived several times. Firefighters testified, "The private enforcement agents threateningly told us to leave them alone. We asked the police for co-operation, but without their assistance, we had to come back every time without putting the fire out." The police turned a blind eye to illegal acts within their cordon and allowed this to go on for eight hours, while using military-grade ballistic shields to protect the enforcement agents who fired water cannons at the protesters.

The truly shocking aspect of the Yongsan disaster was the betrayal of our belief that such brutal deaths and incidents should not occur in twenty-first-century Seoul. We all thought, "we're long past that." We believed such brutal deaths of displaced people were stories of the past, the '60s or '70s. But the Yongsan disaster shed a light on the dark side of Korea's development history, which we, shockingly enough, witnessed in real time.

What has changed about Seoul (and society broadly) in the years since the Yongsan disaster? What has not?
South Korea is an extremely dynamic society. It adapts to the ever-shifting political climate as rapidly as its economy has been growing. This is not to say it doesn't resist injustice or corruption, but there's no denying the side effects of its speedy transformation and growth.

While the Korean constitution includes citizens' right to safety, it doesn't explicitly guarantee protection by the government, instead leaving room for interpretation; many political reformations have prioritized easing restrictions for economic gains and growth rather than ensuring safety, leading to big incidents like the Yongsan disaster.

I would say that the 2014 Sewol ferry disaster brought to light this issue of safety and opened up a real discourse in Korean society. A passenger ferry on its way to Jeju from Incheon sank, taking the lives of 304 people, 250 of whom were Danwon high school students going on a field trip. This incident traumatized a lot of Korean people, and I was no exception. The sentiment spread among us that this could have happened to any one of us, and that no one is safe in this system. Through the trauma and survivor's guilt induced by this disaster, many of us came to deeply empathize with the suffering and better understand the pain and lives of others. Our collective grief taught us our lives are interconnected. The community spirit Korean people showed in their pandemic response and efforts probably had something to do with this hard-learned lesson on interconnectedness and solidarity.

How did the Yongsan tragedy influence the writing of *One Hundred Shadows*?

During the summer and autumn of the year 2009, I worked on *One Hundred Shadows*. Back then, the families of the deceased Yongsan victims were camped out on the first floor of the building where the incident took place, protesting against the city of Seoul and the South Korean government at the time. There was no one held accountable, no official report made available to the public. I spent every day protesting at the site of the incident, and at night, I would come back home to the novel in progress. The shadow of my daytime protests loomed over my novel, sure, but I was extremely careful not to mention the incident directly in my novel. What I did instead was contemplate "the night before," countless times. The very night before the incident, the very place where the incident, that night, had yet to occur, and the people who would have been at a similar place as the one where the incident took place.

The Yongsan disaster cast a long shadow in my life that stretched far beyond the writing of *One Hundred Shadows*. Since my unhappy childhood, I've gotten into the habit of expecting little of the world. Even after I became a novelist, I've always had this sardonic streak that made me think, "The world has always been falling apart, has always been this violent." But all those days I spent interviewing the families of the victims and actively protesting myself changed me. I could no longer live with my former self.

The tipping point for me was when a woman—family to a deceased victim—showed me a memento, the only thing returned from the government. It was a scorched glove sealed in a little plastic bag, and that moment completely shattered my world. Before the woman's distorted face betraying such raw, unfathomable pain, I realized I couldn't continue to explain everything away with my old perspective.

Tell us a bit about how you work. How does a story come to you, and how do you set it on the page?
I don't chase around inspirations or subjects. It's rather that I always have a lot on my mind, and the longer I contemplate, the more likely I'll find myself, at one point, sitting down to write a novel about those contemplations. It's been nineteen years since I started calling myself a novelist, but the world around me never seems to run out of questions and things to think through.

Did you approach this story differently than any of your other projects?
Right up to *One Hundred Shadows*, I've written a lot of books with fantastical elements. For example, I've written about a father who becomes a hat, a lover who turns into a roly-poly, or a door that opens up behind the living and allows for the dead to pass through.

Now, I mostly write realist fiction. The kind of stories I want to tell these days don't call for fantastical conceits. But it's not like I've made up my mind and walked away from fantastical fiction altogether, so I might just pick it up again someday.

Are there any themes or story elements in *One Hundred Shadows* that you would like to continue exploring in future works? What draws you to them?

I've shared much so far, but in truth, *One Hundred Shadows* was born from a very simple wish and written with a very straightforward goal in mind. Most things were beyond my power back when the families of the Yongsan victims felt isolated, those responsible remained silent, and the reality of the incident was nothing but brutal. I decided to write through my feeling of helplessness, whatever book I ended up writing, because that was my job; and even better, I wanted to write something warm, something like a song. The novel, to my own surprise, evolved into a sort of love story. This is one of my most important themes: the resolve to hold on tightly to love, no matter the circumstances.

Thank you for reading this title from Erewhon Books, publishing books that embrace the liminal and unclassifiable and championing the unusual, the uncanny, and the hard-to-define.

We are proud of the team behind *One Hundred Shadows*:

Sarah Guan, Publisher
Diana Pho, Executive Editor
Viengsamai Fetters, Assistant Editor

Martin Cahill, Campaign Manager
Kasie Griffitts, Sales Associate

Cassandra Farrin, Director
Leah Marsh, Production Editor
Kelsy Thompson, Production Editor

Samira Iravani, Art Director
Alice Moye-Honeyman, Junior Designer
Natalie Sousa, Cover Designer

. . . and the whole Kensington Books team!

Learn more about Erewhon Books and our authors at erewhonbooks.com.

Find Erewhon Books on most social media at @erewhonbooks.